LIFE IS RIGHT HERE

MAGDALENA DI SOTRU
SOPHIA SOAMES

ISBN: 9798356579912

ASIN: B0B9192JCH

Cover Design © 2022 Sophia Soames

All artwork and fonts are licensed for commercial use by Sophia Soames, for distribution via electronic media and/or print. Final copy and promotional rights included.

This is a work of fiction. Names, characters, places and incidents are products of the author's imagination or are used fictitiously.

References to real people, events, TV shows, organisations, establishments or locations are intended to provide a sense of authenticity and are used fictitiously. Any resemblance to actual events, locations, organisations or persons, living or dead, is entirely coincidental.

The author acknowledges the copyrighted or trademarked status and trademark owners of the products mentioned in this work.

Beta reading by Karen Meeus Editing

Editing by Debbie McGowan

Proofreading by Suki Fleet

Linguistic advisors: Mary Vitrano (Italian) and Dieter Moitzi (German)

Sensitivity reader: Vin George

"And here you are," he said softly.

"Like you knew I would be."

*We sounded like a bad pop song from our youth.
Or an even worse one from the present.*

Summary

"We're going to have a brilliant Christmas, Andreas. Just like it was ten years ago, all of us together," Vati said, placing steaming cups of coffee in front of us. "We're just pointing out that you and Fredrik always had something special, and you haven't seen each other for years. It will be lovely for you to reconnect."

"Reconnecting is fine. We can discuss college life versus German nursing schools, drink Jägerbombs and watch weird Norwegian shit on TV. Christmas will be thrilling."

"Andreas..." Vati warned as Lottie burst into giggles.

"You adore Fredrik. Still. I can see it in your eyes. You go all panic-stricken and weird when we even mention Freee—"

"Fredrik has a girlfriend in America. Maria hates my guts. Frank and Thomas will whip my butt for not visiting over summer, and anyway, I have to buy them a big present to bribe them to even talk to me."

Vati smiled. "Frank and Thomas love you like a son, and they will just hug the shit out of you as usual."

"Alongside Maria's boyfriend, and Fredrik's girlfriend. It will be a delightful group hug," I snarled.

"Fredrik's girlfriend isn't coming. I told you that," Vati said sternly. He was pissed off with me already, and we hadn't even had breakfast.

"Whatever," I huffed.

Awkward was the word I was looking for. This whole thing was going to be super awkward. Because they always were. And Fredrik? My world used to spin around the strange, blond boy who was my best friend for a few years. He lit up my life. Then he fucked off. Well, he fucked off because I told him to. I was stupid and scared. I think he was too.

Awkward. That wasn't even the start of what this Christmas was going to be like.

Authors' Note

Life is Right Here was intended to be a one-chapter Christmas epilogue to *Life is Good and Other Lies*.

This book is still that, an epilogue, and should be read after *Life is Good and Other Lies* to make sense. We hope that it will bring everything full circle and that you will enjoy, once again, following this family to their final HEA.

Trigger warnings

Terminal and life-threatening illness involving a partner.

Bipolar disorder.

Talk of suicide and the fear of this.

Far too many sugar-laden Christmas foods.

This book has an HEA.

Ten Years Later

Chapter One
Andreas

Okay. This was awkward. Yup. Like...you know when things get super strange over the years and then you suddenly have to grow up and realise that you've spent your teens being a total twat? That was me. Yes. You know. The guy who still thought he was all cool and worldly and in touch with his feelings and all that...imbecilic nonsense.

I blamed my parents for that little personality trait. Completely. You see, my parents were the best. *Sometimes.* Sometimes my Vati was a complete bastard and pushed all my buttons, in the worst way. Sometimes my Papi needed to *not* be so laid-back that he was practically horizontal. My sisters were brats. Me? I was clearly a total fuck-up.

I used to be quite good at all the school stuff and graduated okay. Then my family spent that summer, the one after I graduated, with my parents' best friends. Well, they're family too really. Uncle Thomas and Uncle Frank. We all go on holiday, every damn year. Then we go to Oslo for Christmas, and they come over here for Easter, and then we holiday in summer, and we all go to Oslo Pride and they come here for Berlin Pride, and then... Well, after a particularly embarrassing joint summer holiday, seven years ago, things were never the same. Not for me, anyway.

I crashed and burned that autumn. Couldn't get out of bed. I suddenly hated myself. Hated absolutely everything and everyone. Papi didn't help, even though he's like a super-trained medical person. He let me spend a year locked away in my room gaming and smoking shit I would previously never have gone near. I said I was fine. Papi shrugged. Vati screamed the house down. I gamed. Smoked. Slept. Chilled.

Not that that was a problem, apart from kind of losing a year of my life. I called it a gap year. Papi tried to get me to go to Oslo and get a job. Any job. Experience life. Travel. Go stay with Frank and Thomas. Reconnect with Fredrik and Maria. Vati just stared at me and sighed, kissed my forehead and locked me out of the house until I agreed to let him take me to a therapist.

Yeah. Like that would have worked out. I went to see the therapist, kept my mouth shut, never went back.

The last time I saw Maria, she wanted to kick my skinny arse to kingdom come. She had a point. But then she was also a fully-fledged human who worked full time and spent her holidays doing useful research in Guatemala or someplace, saving the rainforest and campaigning for climate change.

Fredrik. Let's not talk about Fredrik. Because shit like that messed you up.

I had managed, somehow, to complete a degree in behavioural nursing, and I worked, like a grown up, with young adults with varying degrees of neurodivergence. I rotated my shifts between a few group homes, and even though you would think, *it's just a job*, it wasn't. You connected with these people, created bonds and trust, and somehow... Fucking hell, I sounded grown-up, like I kind of meant all those sentences I spouted when I had the monthly meetings with concerned parents and the staff and the kids. Some of them were not kids. I dealt mostly with adults, people who had amazing, full lives despite disabilities that would have crippled the likes of me.

I suppose that made me an adult too. Life had thrown me a plot twist, and without realising, I'd kind of taken it and run with it. I grew up. That realisation was terrifying at times.

I moved away from home, rented a nice flat, missed everyone, decided to take on a few more courses, and then moved back home at the grand old age of twenty-five. Now, two years later, I realised it hadn't been the brightest thing to do, but I'd wanted to buy a flat and was saving up for a deposit, and anyway, Vati and Papi didn't mind, even though Papi kept threatening to turn my old room into a pinball haven. The girls, though, they kept saying I was turning into our dads, and I cringed at the thought.

I'd never wanted to become my parents. Despite how much I loved them, I wasn't them. I never had been and never would be. Neither would my sisters.

Lilly was a brat, a real party girl, out every weekend, barely coming home. She had a menagerie of boyfriends who came and went—the number of times I'd stumbled into the kitchen to find some half-naked guy standing with his head in the fridge drinking milk out of the carton? Animals, all of them. Yeah, that was probably me too, several times over, in my younger days, but anyway.

Lottie spent all her time on Tinder. She was trouble if you asked me, not that my opinion mattered to Lotts, but I felt sorry for the poor guys she hooked up with. She got all excited while I sat there and sighed, watching her scroll through these unsuspecting guys who had no idea that my sister came with standards, ideals. She didn't just expect a date; she expected a lifetime commitment to her world, her future and the future of our planet. So, it was no surprise that she was back on the sofa grumpier than ever this morning when I rolled out into the living room.

"Good date?" I teased, and she did exactly what I expected her to do—rolled her eyes and stuck out her tongue.

"Lilly stayed over at that Axel guy's again."

"Axel?"

"Yeah the short skinny guy who can't stand still."

"The one Vati calls the Duracell bunny?"

"Yeah. She's into him. No idea why."

"I suppose he's cute. If you're into bunnies."

She sighed deeply.

"What was wrong with the guy last night?"

"Just wanted to fuck. Said all the right things and then wanted to know if we were going back to his or mine. I told him to sit and spin."

"You don't give people a chance. Perhaps he's just bad at conversation?"

She stared at me, eyes black with hate. Not that she hated me. I loved my sisters, and they adored me. At least, I think they did. Sometimes.

"You're really coming with us to Oslo for Christmas?"

"Yeah."

"You never come anymore."

"Well, you go every year, and I've been working."

"And now this year you're suddenly not working."

"Nope."

"Got nothing to do with the fact that Fredrik is back from the States, and for the first time in years we'll all be there in person. The whole clan, nobody checking in via FaceTime."

"Nope. Got nothing to do with the threatening emails from Thomas either. He told me he would personally come and escort me from Berlin if I didn't turn up. Sometimes he's more controlling than Vati."

"Vati is not controlling. He'll whip your butt if he hears you say that."

"*I can hear you, you ungrateful brats,*" came from the bedroom across the hall. Vati heard *everything*.

"You're as bad as Thomas when it comes to making me do things I don't want to do," I retaliated, throwing myself down on the sofa with a creak as Vati appeared, still trying to tie his dressing gown belt around his waist.

"Why have you not lit the candles? It's almost Christmas. We have candles. Let's make this place a bit homely." Vati was suddenly scurrying around with his lighter, setting the bloody flat on fire with all his candles.

Lottie huffed. "Just because I'm the only woman around these days, it shouldn't be up to me to make this place liveable. Honestly, Vati, sometimes I feel like I share this flat with a bunch of uni students, not a qualified nurse, a surgeon and a teacher. I mean, look at us."

"Is there coffee?" Vati yelled, now in the kitchen. "None of you made coffee?"

"Where's Papi? Isn't that his job?"

"He was in theatre until two o'clock this morning. Major complications, apparently. They saved someone's life."

"Well done, Papi," I muttered. "He can still get up and make us coffee."

"You can still get up and make us coffee, Andreas." Vati came over and kissed my forehead as he always did. He was still as affectionate as ever, even though all of us were grown up, on paper at least. I shivered with unease every time I realised I was twenty-seven.

"You need to start behaving like adults," he said. "But you can't move out. Or get married. Or have kids. I'm not becoming a granddad yet. I'm not ready for babies. Use condoms."

"Yes, Vati, dear. Responsible sex. We know."

"How was your date, Lottie?" he asked, smothering Lottie in kisses.

"Or no sex." Lottie sighed. "He was just like the others, Vati. An arse."

"But you spoke to him on the phone and said he was nice."

"He *was* nice. Not right. It needs to be right."

"You can have casual sex, Lotts. It's not forbidden," I inserted like the nice big brother I was.

"I don't like casual sex. I want commitment. I want a boyfriend. I want someone to share my life with. Lilly can do the casual sex all she wants, but it's not for me. Well, sometimes it is, but no. Not this guy."

"That's fine, sweetie," Vati said and hurried back to the kitchen.

He was funny, and Lottie and I shared a brief giggle. Vati was the one who told us to talk openly about sex in the house, then he ran off and hid when we did. As if he hadn't heard it all by now. I'd even told him about my catastrophic threesome. Papi had laughed so much I'd been worried he would have a heart attack over dinner, yet Vati couldn't look me in the eyes for days after. Not my fault. He asked. I told.

"Do you and Fredrik even message each other anymore?" Lottie asked.

"He's happy with his girlfriend. Apparently."

"You're still his friend."

"He's like at some big college doing his second master's or something and plays American football and is all worldly. I still live at home and can't find anyone who wants to be with me."

"You're just boring and grumpy."

"I'm hot and educated. I just don't think dating and hook-ups work for me. I want to come back to my own bed at night and sleep."

"You can still hook up with people. That's normal. Just get yourself laid once in a while and you'll be all happy and satisfied. Why are you complaining?"

"I'm not complaining. It's just not my thing."

"No, your thing is Fredrik. We all know. Your first love."

"Shut up, Lotts."

"So, for the first time in like a million years, the great mystery that is Andreas is coming back to Oslo for Christmas."

"I have spent plenty of Christmases in Oslo."

"Remember the first year, when Frank had that big episode and we ended up on our own in the house and had this brilliant Christmas party. Thomas was with Frank at the hospital, and Papi was running Vati backwards and forwards. We had the best parent-free Christmas ever."

"Frank was really unwell, Lotts. It wasn't all fun."

"No, but he'd made all that food and we lived like kings for days. Remember that snowball fight we had in the garden in the middle of the night? Oh. Those sweets. He's promised to make me a whole jar of butter toffees to take home this year."

"Frank loves you, Lotts. You've always been his favourite. He even did German DuoLingo so he could speak to you properly when you couldn't speak English."

"He still texts me in German. It's kind of sweet."

"Anyway, I came that year when we all went skiing."

"Yeah, that was fun. You and Fredrik had stopped speaking to each other and Maria kept calling you Idiot one and Idiot two."

"Then I came the year after."

"Yeah, because Fredrik was in America. It was the most drama-free Christmas in Oslo ever."

"We went to that Christmas play at the theatre, and you both fell asleep."

"It was in flipping Norwegian. Of course I fell asleep!"

"The ice-skating is always fun. And the mulled wine."

"Thomas gets us all drunk on the first night. It's tradition. There are Jägerbombs poured before we even have our boots off."

"Vati is so funny when he's drunk."

"We should get him drunk more often."

"*I can hear you!!*" came from the kitchen.

"So, you're all chill with seeing the love of your life again? After all these years?"

"Lottie..."

"You'll take one look at him, all muscular and blond and handsome, and then you'll jump him and maul him in the hallway, dry-humping the poor dude in front of his parents."

"I'm not gay, Lottie. And I am not in love with Fredrik."

"Fuck off, Andreas."

"I'm serious! It's some kind of fucked-up thing in this family, all of you trying to make me all gay with Fredrik all of the time."

"See? Hit a nerve?"

"Calm down, Lottie," Vati said, placing steaming cups of coffee in front of us. "We're going to have a brilliant Christmas, Andreas. Just like it was ten years ago, all of us together. We're just pointing out that you and Fredrik always had something special, and you haven't seen each other for years. It will be lovely for you to reconnect."

"Reconnecting is fine. We can discuss college life versus German nursing schools, drink Jägerbombs and watch weird Norwegian shit on TV. Christmas will be thrilling."

"Andreas..." Vati warned as Lottie burst into giggles.

"You adore Fredrik. Still. I can see it in your eyes. You go all panic-stricken and weird when we even mention Freee—"

"Fredrik has a girlfriend in America. Maria hates my guts. Frank and Thomas will whip my butt for not visiting over summer, and anyway, I have to buy them a big present to bribe them to even talk to me."

Vati smiled. "Frank and Thomas love you like a son, and they will just hug the shit out of you as usual."

"Alongside Maria's boyfriend, and Fredrik's girlfriend. It will be a delightful group hug," I snarled.

"Fredrik's girlfriend isn't coming. I told you that," Vati said sternly. He was pissed off with me already, and we hadn't even had breakfast.

"Whatever," I huffed.

Awkward was the word I was looking for. This whole thing was going to be super awkward. Because they always were. And Fredrik? My world used to spin around the strange, blond boy who was my best friend for a few years. He lit up my life. Then he fucked off. Well, he fucked off because I told him to. I was stupid and scared. I think he was too.

Awkward. That wasn't even the start of what this Christmas was going to be like.

Chapter Two
Fredrik

I WAS GOING home. *Home alone.* The phrase reminded me of an old movie my dad loved. Thomas, for anyone wondering. Frank couldn't stand the actor in that movie for some reason. Nobody ever understood why.

I graduated a few years ago, with a prestigious degree in Particle Physics, my diploma thesis written without inspiration, about some theoretical problem nobody but a hardcore academic would ever find any use for, to get it over with. And no, I was not depressed. Thomas had asked me several times, and I was pretty sure I was not, nor ever had been, depressed on any clinical scale. I was just tired of it all. The career runs. The aspiration for more. The encouragement to be the best, to achieve, to keep aiming higher. The awards and prizes and competitions. The *winner takes it all* and the American dream. Nobody could ever finish last, failure never an option.

"But you have to be polite and let someone else be last," Frank had told me this one time he'd had to pick me up early from school. I'd been told off, and then my teacher had complained to Frank about my distracted slow pace in the cloakroom every time our class went out during the breaks, when I was always the last to put my coat on. I'd been in first grade back then. I still remembered my teacher's sour face.

"She looked like Maria did when she was tasting lemons," I'd told Frank in the warm, dry car on our way home. The rain had drummed in a steady stream against the windows. My grey jeans had been wet and cold against my skin, and a bag stuffed with wet rain gear was in the trunk. That had been the problem. My friend Petter and I had lain down in a pond-like puddle in the schoolyard to see if our rain gear would hold out. It hadn't passed the test. We'd both been soaked, and our teacher had been fuming.

I didn't know why I remembered this. Maybe it was the weather outside the dull shuttle bus to LAX, the unusual low clouds drizzling rain, stripes of water running along the side windows. It was the last time I was travelling home from America now, and even LA was crying actual tears. I wasn't coming back. Or if I did, it would be for a holiday, or *vacation*, as my US-English-honed brain corrected me. From now on, things would always be different. This used to be my home, and now it was not, the last seven years all packed up in a backpack. Mostly clothes, a few other things. My laptop was in my carry-on bag. I could probably have charmed the backpack into the cabin, too, to speed things up at the other end, but I couldn't be bothered. I didn't feel like smiling at strangers today. I just wanted to slide through the airport like an anonymous man, someone who didn't care, someone who wasn't cared for. I just wanted to go home for Christmas.

Bringing Emily back with me had never been part of the plan, yet Thomas had asked twice if I was sure she wouldn't come with me. Of course she wouldn't. She was never going to leave her all-American family in New Mexico, and she was definitely not being invited after Thomas told me Andreas would accompany Gabriel and Bruno this year, for the first time in who knew how long. Scratch that. I knew perfectly well how long. Seven years. Seven Christmases. Or six Christmases after the one I'd skipped.

I'd moved to Boston that autumn. No, I'd fled. I hadn't admitted it before, but that was what I'd done. I'd finished my second year at NTNU in Trondheim, planning an exchange term after Christmas. I'd researched German universities. Berlin, Essen, Bonn, Göttingen, Hamburg— NTNU had lots of exchange agreements, and I, somehow, had managed perfect scores through my first two years of mathematics and physics, so being accepted would be a triviality, especially as I had just passed my Goethe-Zertifikat at B2-level. Nobody knew that, though, not after I decided to ditch all my mistakes and pretty much run away. My tutor had sounded surprised when I called him during his summer vacation and begged him to help me get an exchange somewhere else, right now, anywhere. I hadn't said why and he hadn't asked when I'd broken down in his office a few days later. He'd just nodded and talked to some colleagues. A week later, I was sweating over my motivational letter for Boston University.

I was accepted immediately—my tutor had a big hand in that—and I'd left Norway just days before my third year was due to start, barely dropping in at home to dump my stuff before heading to the USA. My dads were worried, curious and torn about my sudden change of plans, but I'd said it was just an opportunity that had fallen into my lap, an open door that was too good to pass. Nobody argued with that, of course. My dad, Thomas, knew his academia.

Maria, with her own juggling of studies and student activities at the student society in Trondheim, saw straight through me and tried to interrogate me about what had happened. She talked to Andreas—well, more like she shouted at him on a weekly basis and called him names—and claimed he'd told her everything, but it was just a trick to get me to spill the gossip. He wouldn't have said anything about what had happened; I knew what he was like, even if I didn't know him as well as I'd thought I had.

My dads cried when I left. They wanted me to stay for a few days, to come home for fall break. They would pay for my tickets so I could go with them to Sweden or Germany or England or Spain or wherever they were going that autumn.

Well, France, actually. I knew the exact address and exterior and interior of the Airbnb house they'd rented in Figeac, a town located between Montpellier and Bordeaux. I knew how they would allocate the two large bedrooms with king-size beds overlooking the valley—morning sun and view for the parents at one end, my twin sisters at the other. Wine, food, pool, chilling, long dinners, more wine.

There were also two rooms in the attic of that house, far away from everyone else, or at least a creaky flight of spiral stairs away. The attic's narrow windows still provided a beautiful view, and there was a shared bathroom between the rooms, both of them identically equipped with a queen-size bed, wardrobe and desk. Andreas and I would have chosen a room each but would have ended up in the one to the left of the bathroom because it had the bed to the right of the door, which was how my room in Oslo was, our one stable point in the universe, the place we'd always met since that first visit to Aunt Bella's house where my dads still spent a lot of time.

Until that summer.

By the following autumn, I'd been a successful student in Boston. I ended up completing my degree there, but instead of applying for the PhD program, I worked a bit, travelled a bit, settled in California and applied for a PhD in environmental physics at UCSB. The years there now were kind of a haze. There had been Emily, of course. But before her, there was Jennifer, Eric, Christina, Jamie, Shamil…and a string of faceless hook-ups that I'd shamefully tucked away in my memories.

I'd tried. I *really* had tried. My dads had been together since they were in their twenties, a lifetime. We all knew the story about how they'd met and found love and lost and found and lost and found and then never lost again. It was like a fairy tale, like one of Frank's favourite movies, even if Thomas kept teasing him that their meet-cute wasn't actually an epic love story of any sort. He always said it had been fate. Thing was, I'd always wanted that for myself, and I'd thought Andreas had been the one, back when we were teenagers. But then he wasn't, and I didn't know what I'd done wrong or why anything had happened in the first place.

My flights home to Oslo this time were chaotic and stressful with too many people going somewhere for Christmas. I'd managed to wrap myself into my own bubble of blankets and cheap pillows and dozed over Canada, then watched the ice over Greenland in wide-eyed, jet-lagged wonder. I'd barely registered landing in Paris before rushing through CDG, a mishmash of then-futuristic architecture from the last century and modern, energy-saving solutions that made me dizzy. I barely caught my flight and dozed off again the second I hit my seat. I felt calmer now; home was getting closer. *If it was still home*, I thought before my brain shut off.

"Fredrik!" My dad's arms were long and warm around me outside customs. I dropped my bag and backpack on the floor. My eyes were wet; my god, how much I had missed him. I leant into his chest and inhaled the familiar smell of his shampoo and aftershave, the detergent we used at home, his stubble scratching my cheek, his hair tickling my lips. I breathed him in for who knew how long. Seconds, minutes, I didn't care.

I was finally home again.

"Where's Thomas?" I asked when Frank let go of me. He scrunched his nose when I dried my tears with the back of my hand, a well-known smile on his lips. Even though I'd seen him on videocalls every week, it was still a shock to the system to see him up close. My handsome, vibrant father looked a million years old, even with the colourful beanie on his head and his jacket zipped up tight. The clothes didn't hide the fact that he was thin as a rake and pale as a ghost, nor that he'd slumped down on a bench as soon as I let go of him.

"Here!" Another set of arms hooked me up from behind and locked around my chest and upper arms. I laugh-wrestled to get him off me, knowing exactly where to tickle him to make him fall on the ground in seconds. If I could just get my hand behind and up...

"Nope," he laughed while holding me tighter. "I know what you're up to, and I'm not letting you do that."

Frank sat there laughing. "Stay calm, Fredrik," he said while trying to stand up again. "Your old man is not a youngster anymore. We're all about dodgy body parts and tired legs these days!"

Thomas released me and chuckled. "Sit down, Frank. Don't exhaust yourself. We still have to walk back to the car. But maybe we should behave like adults since we're apparently three adults here now." He looked me up and down. "You've grown, son." His voice was low and raspy, somehow sounding more mature yet so familiar. He cleared his throat, trying to hold back his emotions.

For a minute, we were all silent, giving me a chance to gather all the thoughts in my head. "Come on, Dads, don't get all sappy. Take me home and feed your long-lost son a piglet. I'm starving."

"I think it was a calf you ate last time," Frank mumbled. "Thomas half emptied the supermarket the other day, buying enough food to feed our incoming army."

"Army," I muttered as the reminder of what was still to come punched me in the stomach. One gut punch after the other, Frank took my arm, needing my help to get up onto his feet.

"Doesn't matter. Maria's probably made something vegetarian anyway." Thomas laughed. "You *will* get fed. Don't worry."

Frank stopped in his tracks and shrugged. "What about us making a pit stop at that McDonald's before heading home? I haven't had a burger for ages. I think I might manage one. Or has California turned you vegetarian too, Fredrik?"

"Nope. No way." I thought it was a perfect idea. I needed food, calm, normality.

"Okay, Mækkern, it is," Thomas said.

***

"So Emma didn't come with you?" Thomas asked as we munched our way through piles of greasy fries and a chicken burger each. *Organic, free-range, climate-neutral,* according to the posters. It was a decade too late, and we all felt a bit ashamed about stuffing our faces with meat, but we had a mostly vegetarian Christmas ahead, now all the Fischer-Morettis had gone green.

"I guess we'll have to order takeaway burgers for sneak-eating in the garage," Frank suggested with a smile, "since we're all about the environment now. This Emma, is she a vegetarian too?"

"Emily," I corrected him. "No, and no. I already told you, didn't I? We're friends. Nothing more, nothing less." I was well aware that I sounded like a grumpy teen. Oh, how easily things slipped back into place. Or back in time. I wasn't sure which.

"I just thought—" Thomas began.

"There's nothing to think about, Dad. She was never going to come with me. End of story."

"Okay, okay." He held up his hands in peace. "Just asking."

"Yeah, sure," I muttered, trying to calm down.

"So is there someone—"

"Thomas!" Frank's voice was thick with warning.

"Sorry." Thomas shook his head. "If you don't want to talk about it, you only have to say so."

"No."

"Sorry."

"No, I mean, there is nobody. Can we just not talk about my love life now? I've been travelling for a day, I'm hungry and tired, and my head is spinning. I just want to go to bed."

He put his hand on mine. "Sorry, son. What do you want? I can grab you some more food." He looked around as if to check for an imaginary waitress when the only worker in this joint was taking orders behind the counter. My gaze wandered to the sickening sundae poster on the screen behind them. It had way too much of everything.

"I'm not hungry."

"Oh, I thought you said..." He tilted his head and studied me.

"I think we're ready to go home now." Frank's statement was stern and directed at Thomas, who stood up and started to clear our trays, wrappers and bamboo cutlery.

Suddenly I felt like I couldn't move a single muscle anymore. My brain was goading me on, but my body just sat there, my arms dangling, my feet seemingly glued to the ground.

Frank had to help me up and lead me out, holding my hand like I was still a small child. The smell of him lingered in my nose after he secured me in the back of the car behind Thomas, in the driver's seat. Frank took the passenger seat beside him. I fell asleep with his eyes watching me through the rear-view mirror while heavy snow fell in the outside darkness.

***

The next morning, I was woken by Maria's loud voice and the mattress sagging as she sat on the edge of my bed. "Hey. You've slept for fifteen hours, you kind of have to get up now. There's no way you can still be tired. Seriously. Coffee?"

The smell of the brew had already hit my nostrils, that wonderful roasted smell with the seasonal spices she loved to add to whatever brew our parents were currently drinking—cinnamon and vanilla for Christmas, orange peel for Easter, berries for summer. Sometimes we tormented her, suggesting she should switch to tea, at which she would growl. She might have removed a lot from her diet with her ridiculous fads, but coffee was not something any of us had been able to give up.

I shuffled into a sitting position and reached for the mug; a few sips later, I felt human again. It happened so fast I never got to experience the sleepy haze of waking up, going through the bathroom routine, getting dressed and finally ending up in the kitchen making coffee. I'd thought numerous times I should have bought a coffee machine for my dorm room, but in all those years I'd never got around to it.

"Can you serve me my coffee every morning?" I asked.

"Huh?" She scrunched her forehead.

"It's a nice way to wake up—no break between sleep and coffee. Can you do that every day? It's either that or getting an IV line installed. I'll ask Bruno." I grinned, fully aware that placing demands on my sister was a sure path to never again getting spoiled like this with coffee in bed.

"In your dreams," she muttered. "But it is good to have you back."

She crawled into my bed and pulled the blanket up over her pyjama-clad legs. "So, what's the plan?" No beating around the bush with Maria.

I was, in a way, grateful for that, although her question had startled me, and I hissed in pain as I quickly swallowed the mouthful of too-hot coffee.

"Good thing we're not in the States or I'd have to sue you for burning my tongue with your dangerously hot coffee."

"Good thing I'm a coffee purist and wouldn't dream of adding cold water to your brew to cool it to a safe temperature for your fragile tongue."

I laughed at her. Everything was like it used to be between us, which was a relief. The past months had been kind of awkward. We hadn't talked much, too busy to match our schedules, so it had been asynchronous chats, a single question or a full monologue from one of us, the answer coming hours or days later. On the rare occasions we were free at the same time, we'd sit there for half an hour, sending short phrases back and forth, finishing each other's thoughts. People said twins had a special bond, and sometimes it felt like they might be right. But while Maria and I had a close sibling bond, we hadn't talked about the things that mattered. The cloud hanging above us was large and very obvious, yet we still didn't dare address it.

"Are you ready for Andreas coming tomorrow then?" she asked instead.

I spluttered my coffee all over the beige bed linen. "Fuck."

"Exactly."

"See what you did? These sheets were clean and now there's coffee everywhere!"

She handed me some tissues from the box on my bedside table. "Because I asked if you're ready for Andreas?"

I sighed. "I guess I am ready for our visitors, but it would've been nice for once for it to only be the four of us. Like a regular family, you know?"

"They *are* family."

"A blood family then. You know what I mean."

She didn't comment on my exclusion of one of our dads there, even though it was something we'd fought over and used as daggers in the past. We were both Thomas's biological children. We'd only found out a few years back, and that little omission had caused a fair bit of drama. Not that it mattered, but our dads should've told us when we were kids instead of us finding out through a stupid Ancestry.com bloody DNA test we'd done for fun.

"We've been celebrating Christmas with them for, like, ten years," she said. "Why not this year?"

"Because I haven't been home for ages, and maybe I'd like some time with only you and our dads."

Maria looked at me like she had all the patience in the world when I knew she didn't. Her green eyes pierced into me, probing my brain for answers. She should have become a police interrogator instead of a physics teacher. At least she would always succeed at getting the kids to tell the truth when they were cheating on their exams or whatever.

"Fuck off, Maria." I averted my gaze to the coffee stain on the sheet, studying it like it was one of those ink blots that supposedly reveal all kinds of stuff about your psyche, but all I saw was a splotch of coffee. Maybe that was me, my life. Carelessly spilling my coffee and my chances.

I opened my mouth to speak but swallowed to make the words go away and instead pressed my lips together until they hurt against my teeth.

"Okay," Maria said after what felt like an eternity. She got out of the bed, leaving a cold, gaping hole, and closed the door behind her with a quiet click.

I swallowed again. Swallowed everything I'd wanted to spill to Maria—about Andreas, Emily, America, my dreams, my nightmares. And the fact that my dad was dying and there was nothing in the world I could do to stop it.

Chapter Three
Andreas

It DIDN'T GET better just because we were on Norwegian soil. I still felt like a fraud, despite the girls' obvious excitement over the snow on the train platform as we stumbled out into the darkness that loomed even though it was early afternoon.

Lottie was climbing a pile of grey mush, her bags carelessly thrown on the ground as Papi struggled to fit his usually well-packed and dutifully declared crate of German beer on top of his suitcase. Vati was paying for our travelcards on the app and swearing loudly in German, and Lilly and I were making snowballs and throwing them at each other. The madness that was our family. Unlike normal people, we couldn't travel anywhere without making a big song and dance about it. People were staring, and rightly so. We were five adults behaving like kids in the middle of Oslo Central station. Vati shouted at us to follow him as we all rumbled out onto the main square, where the trams thundered past full of late Christmas shoppers and other stressed-out humans who didn't need some deranged Germans standing in their way.

"I can smell the sea!" Lottie shouted. "I need to find myself a nice Norwegian man so I can move here and live here forever!" She sang it with her arms outstretched while Papi pretended he didn't know us.

Long gone were the days when we were met with signs and a welcome wagon at the airport. These days, we knew our way and all happily got on the right tram, stealing seats and piling our bags next to Papi, who as always, volunteered to stand up for others needing the seats. Unlike his spoiled brat kids, who were actually not kids anymore.

"You're not on Tinder already, are you?" I hissed at Lilly, who was scrolling through some unsuspecting blokes' profiles on her phone.

"Look. Bisexual man looking for a third. Something for you, 'Dreas?" She batted her eyelashes at me, like she didn't know that everyone on the bus was now staring at me, or the ones who understood German, at least.

"Shut it, Lils."

I just wanted to sit here in peace and quiet. It was all I'd have for a while with all these crazies around me, and I was not going to freak out over a certain someone being there. I just wouldn't allow myself to. See? I could be chill. Totally relaxed. I would just shake his hand and talk about the weather. *How's life been treating you, old fellow?* That kind of thing. I dealt with people every day; I could surely deal with my ex.

My ex. I hated thinking about him like that. He was...well, I couldn't even describe it in my head. He was just this kid who had made me see the world in a different way. Younger than me but had his shit together. He knew what he liked, and yeah, he liked me. I liked him too. I mean, we became the best of friends during a stupid summer holiday, and then we went camping and we kind of...made out.

That should have been the end of it—something we laughed about and wrote off as a funny thing we did in our youth. Instead, it just went on, like an out-of-control speeding train. He texted me every day, and I texted him back. If he didn't text, I would panic and ring him, and then after a while we talked every night. Then we talked every morning too. Then I saw him again, and let's just say there was a reason the girls still teased me about mauling him in the hallway in front of his parents. That one was all on me. I had no idea what had got into the eighteen-year-old me, but I'd launched at him and eaten his face in front of Uncle Frank and Uncle Thomas, so I hadn't only kissed Fredrik. I'd gone full-on gay on him.

I'd drifted off completely by the time Vati tugged at my jacket to get me off the tram. We walked up the now-familiar road lined with pretty houses, twinkling Christmas lights everywhere, candle arches in windows and warm star lights. It was all very festive and cheerful—and clean and bright, especially with the snow covering everything in sight. We got snow in Berlin, but not like this. There were piles and piles of it, and there were still some stray snowflakes whirling past me as I rubbed the snot running from my nose on my gloves. Proper woollen ones gifted from our gracious hosts every time we rocked up here in our apparently unsuitable German winter gear. It didn't matter what we wore, Thomas would mock us mercilessly for our bad winter clothes and then whip out a bag from the wardrobe and ensure we all had the latest high-tech breathable, multifunctional gloves and the warmest hats known to humankind. Everything was better in Norway anyway. His words, and nobody ever dared to disagree. You didn't mess with Uncle Thomas, and I'd known better than to reject his invitation this year.

"You okay, kid?" Papi asked as he caught up and nudged my shoulder. "Need a Man-to-Man talk?"

"Nah," I slobbered back, my nose still running. Trust me to come down with a cold for Christmas. "I'm good."

"I'm here if you need a freak-out," Papi whispered and winked.

"Not having a freak-out," I muttered back.

"Yes, you are, and it's okay. Just drag him out for a beer somewhere public and let it all out."

"That will drain my savings in one go, and I'll have to spend the rest of this holiday at home doing nothing. I'm not going to a Norwegian bar with Fredrik. Nope. Not happening."

It wasn't, and *still* my heart swelled when I saw the house, a place of so many happy moments, of Christmas cheer, of laughter and…yes, all my memories. I needed to make new ones, Lottie had helpfully suggested. She'd promised to find me a nice Norwegian hook-up. *Grindr or Tinder? What do you fancy?* She'd said like it was a totally normal suggestion. I hadn't even known how to answer that. To be honest, I was constantly too confused to care.

Right now, though? I wasn't confused at all.

On the large steps outside the house stood this man, and I had to stop walking before I fell over my own feet. He was way taller than I remembered, and broader, with a fine dusting of stubble on his chin—I could tell because it was covered in frost that glittered in the light from the doorway. His hair was longer than I remembered too, falling in soft waves under his hat, and of course he had been shovelling snow like some elf-ish creature, which would impress my parents no end, not to mention putting him in his dads' good books.

"Fredrik!" the girls shouted in unison, dumping their bags in the middle of the road so they could simultaneously tackle the dude on the steps to the ground. My sisters might've been pretty and elegant, but they were still feral monsters. The three of them were in a pile on the steps as Fredrik—everyone always called him Fredrik, except me—fake-screamed for them to get off him. Well, my Vati was trying to get in there to hug the poor guy too, and Papi was, as always, filming it all on his phone while I stood there like a fool wishing the ground could just swallow me up.

I'd lied when I said I was ready because I was honestly nowhere near ready for this.

Deep breaths. In, out. I realised I was doing that breathing thingy I taught my patients to do at the group home. *In, out. Let's gather ourselves up. There is no panic here. No fear. In, out.*

"Andreas."

I couldn't say a word.

"Welcome back. Good to see you, man." He spoke with that stupid-sounding American twang he had going on. Too much time abroad, obviously. The twat. He reached out to shake my hand.

"Good to see you too, Fredrik," I managed to say, grabbing his gloved hand with my own. I shook it. Tried to smile.

I bloody full-named him. He'd always been *my Freddie*, but he wasn't anymore. Now he was some handsome bastard with an accent and a firm handshake, and I hated him.

"Let me show you to your room," he said and turned his back on me like we were strangers. Like I hadn't spent months and months of my teenage years here in this very house. Like I didn't know this place, these roads, this path to the front door, as well as he did.

This used to be my happy place. The place where my shoes went on the second shelf to the left, where my coat hung on the green peg and Freddie's on the red one. Maria had the blue one. The twins got pink ones a year down the line.

The house where my room was always his, and even when he wasn't there anymore, I'd still slept in his bed.

Not this time.

He pointed at the stairs leading down to the basement. "You're in Frank's office. He made up a blow-up bed on the floor for you." Then he nodded and walked off like I was some kind of unwanted cousin.

It got better. Well, maybe less awkward. Nobody could be mad or upset when Uncle Frank was around, however frustrated I may have been feeling on the inside. Uncle Frank was like sunshine on steroids on a good day, but even on a day like today, when he was a little stressed and obviously hadn't slept at all if you gauged the dark circles under his eyes, he still hugged me like he never wanted to let me go.

"Uncle Frank," I hissed, trying not to be strangled to death.

"My long-lost son!" he declared dramatically and laughed that belly laugh that only Frank could pull off. "You're back. Finally! Thomas said he would actually make good on his threats to go get you himself if you didn't turn up. He even googled flights last night. It would've cost a bit, and then some, but he would've had you back here in time for breakfast tomorrow. Luckily, your Vati assured us you were on the plane this morning, otherwise there'd have been trouble."

"Let the kid go, Frank," Uncle Thomas said and gave me one of his awkward-dad hugs. Thomas was the king of the awkward-dad hug, but he still managed to make me feel all soppy when he whispered, "Good to have you back," in my ear. I think, in spite of everything, Uncle Thomas loved me. He'd hated on me big time for a while, but he'd never said a thing. Never ranted at me. Never cried like Uncle Frank did. Never shut me out of his life like someone else I knew.

Freddie had disappeared and Maria turned up right on time to pull me in for a hug while she whispered all kinds of foul swear words into my neck. I made out *wanker* and *arse wipe* and *drittsekk* and a few other choice Norwegian words before I called her *bitch* and she boxed me in the stomach, which was kind of her. We'd had worse times, but she was still smiling and kissed my cheek and then hugged me again.

"I don't know if I want to give you a black eye or hug the hell out of you," she said softly, her hair much longer and falling in curls over her shoulders. She looked good. Great even. Tanned and healthy with that sparkle in her eyes.

"I'm sorry," I said because I didn't know what else to say right now. I loved Maria. She was the missing piece of my puzzle of sisters, the one that slotted in right between the twins. The stable clever girl who made me feel tiny and useless with a few choice words but who could also steer me right and had, despite everything, always loved me, even if she hadn't called me by my real name for a couple of years. She called me whatever her choice of insult was on the day. I called her selected ones back.

"Motherfucker," I said, grabbing her shoulders. "I bloody love you."

"Fuck off." She grinned but tears pooled in her eyes. See? I still had my touch with her.

"I'm trying to be serious here," I said, even though I couldn't stop smiling because she was simply awesome.

"Stop trying to charm me, Twatfeatures. I will never marry you. We all know that ship sailed when we were teens. Also, you still smell funny, and my god, do you actually ever shave?"

There she was. The snarky Maria I knew and loved. She had both hands around my face, scratching my stubble while smacking kisses on my eyelids and then shaking my shoulders like she wanted to slap me.

"I still hate you," she said with a pout, "but you're here, and that is an A for effort. Well done. I might let you have your Christmas present."

"I might let you have yours—if you can be nice to me for once. Say, call me by my proper name and not call me Wanker over Christmas dinner."

"I can't promise anything, but if you're good, I might wrap Fredrik up with a bow and—"

"Shut up!" I hissed in panic. I could take the teasing and the banter, but not about that. I should have been used to it by now. It wasn't the first time we'd all been together since...well. I just couldn't. Not when I had no idea where I stood and what we were doing and how we were actually going to play this thing out.

"Don't worry. Fredrik told us we're not allowed to make comments or make him feel uncomfortable just because the guy who took his virginity is staying with us for Christmas." Maria smiled sweetly, and Lottie sprayed her drink in a well-aimed shower across the room before Lilly hit her and Thomas said something I couldn't make out and everyone was laughing.

Which I took as my cue to disappear for a while.

I sat in Uncle Frank's office with all his posters and drawings and books, staring at the line of awards sitting on the desk. He did good, our Uncle Frank. He was quite famous and celebrated for a while after a string of well-received documentaries based on Aunt Bella's diaries. They even had real actors in them, acting out some key scenes, which meant we had two people pretend-shagging in the barn at the farm, and it had been awkward as hell watching it all on the big screen. It had been even worse watching the big budget movie that had followed, despite us all being in it as extras. I remember Freddie and I being totally bummed at not even having our names in the credits and Maria calling us stupid. Watching yourself on screen was not all it was hyped up to be, we'd all agreed on that.

Anyway. Uncle Frank had won awards. Maria got interviewed on TV. Uncle Thomas was proud as punch. There was even a framed picture on the desk, the four of them all in dinner suits, even Maria. They all had matching ties. The photo for some reason had me in hysterics, sitting there on my own. Things were weird, and I wished I could just go back home, forget this Christmas even existed. There was another photo of the nine of us all in ski gear. Austria, a few years ago. Then one of the twins. And Maria's graduation photo. A faded paper printout of a younger version of Freddie and me. I felt like ripping it down, with unexplainable anger brewing inside of me. I didn't know why, when this one was all on me. Every single little bit.

I was a grown man now. A responsible man with a responsible job. I had degrees. Certificates with my full name on them. I could surely behave like an adult.

Well, apparently not, as I stomped back upstairs and let my feet carry me down the well-trodden path through the kitchen, past everyone laughing and trying to hand me steamy, spiked wine in a cup. Drinking alcohol now would be the worst decision ever, especially since I stomped down the back hallway and swung his door open, walked in like I owned the place and slammed the door shut behind me.

Chapter Four
Fredrik

"WHAT THE HECK?"

I scrambled around the bed trying to get my spinning head under control. I'd been glaring at my laptop screen, not sure what I'd actually been watching, when the door had swung open. It had taken all of my self-control and energy not to throw myself at him when he'd stood in front of me at the front steps, after Lottie and Lilly were done hugging and I'd brushed the snow off and hugged Gabriel and Bruno. I loved them all to pieces, the best bonus family anyone could ever have had.

And then he'd been there, right in front of me, and all I'd been able to think about was his soft skin, the hollow spot between his collarbones, his muscles under my hands as I stroked across his back, his cheek against mine. He looked really tired. If I could only hold him...

I'd given him my hand instead. His had felt stiff against my cold, wet glove. I'd shaken it once, twice, then I'd let go, because if I hadn't, I would never have been able to.

He'd smiled without looking me in the eyes. I tried...tried not to... I honestly didn't know what I'd tried, so I'd just turned around.

"Let me show you to your room."

I'd walked towards our heavily decorated doorway without checking to see if he was following, painfully aware that the others were watching us, listening in. I shouldn't have cared, but I did. And at that moment, I would have done anything to erase the past ten years of my life.

The rainbow-coloured lights had been angrily flashing around the door. They didn't match the big Santa figure or the traditional wreath Dad always bought from the local craft association. Last year, the decorations had been modest. This year, Frank had gone all out, a thick, green wreath with a silver bow and a few pinecones scattered. Nice and traditional, as the airline magazine no doubt would have described the style. Not that I'd read those magazines, but I'd been jet-lagged and sleep-deprived, and my books had been in my carry-on in the compartment above my head, protected by a large, snoring man sitting between me and the aisle. I read a load of crap on that plane. Watched some really bad movies. Anything to stop me thinking.

We'd both kicked off our shoes inside the door by reflex, mine ending up in a pile of winter boots next to the door, while Andreas' landed next to his sisters' before he picked them up and put them on a shelf. The whole thing made me feel nauseous with longing for a time when things had been happy and carefree. Instead, I'd shivered as I hung my wet coat in the drying cabinet. After living in Boston with virtually no options for drying clothes besides in the washer/dryer, I really valued this apparatus—which had been an insane thought to even think as I stood there, but I couldn't help it. I was lost, and out of the corner of my eye I'd seen Andreas move a jacket from one of the pegs on the other wall before hanging his own on the peg that had always been his.

Frank had argued that Andreas should sleep in my room, like he always used to. It would be impolite to make him feel unwelcome by housing him somewhere else, he'd said, when I'd suggested a nearby hotel. I'd cringed even saying it, but Andreas had always used my bed even when I'd been away. I'd said no, no way, and had another furious moment when Dad had the audacity to suggest I could sleep in his office in the basement while Andreas took my bed. He'd sighed and sent Thomas downstairs to pull out the air bed from the storage room. "We need to get a sofa bed for my office," I'd heard him tell Thomas as he'd passed through the kitchen before his voice disappeared back downstairs.

"You're in Frank's office. He made up a blow-up bed on the floor for you." I'd pointed Andreas towards the basement. The last I'd seen of him was his slumped shoulders as he walked down the stairs, heavy, reluctant steps, as if he was on his way to death row. "Dead man walking," had been on my tongue, but it was too morbid; he wasn't dead, not even to me. He was just a boy—no. A man. A man my family knew, a family guest. Nothing more.

Albeit still the most gorgeous man, his unruly hair a little too long, dressed in jeans and a shirt that had seen better days. The look was so comfortingly familiar that once again I wanted to cry.

So why the heck was he standing here, on my rug, next to my bed, two steps to the right of the door, on the spot where he'd stood so many times that whenever I'd come home it had been weird *not* seeing him there? Why was he standing here as if he owned the place, like he was about to push my stuff to the side to make room for his own things? And most importantly, why was he looking at me with rage in his eyes, ready to kill me?

"Fuck it, Freddie! We can't go on like this! We need to talk. We're adults now. We've grown up and graduated and have proper jobs—at least, I do— and we can't mope around like stupid kids just because we were once in love and still, here I am, throwing a tantrum because you broke up with me seven years ago and we didn't agree on anything so we stopped talking as if it was some kind of high school drama! We can't be like this all Christmas. I'm gonna go crazy..." He stopped to allow himself to breathe, and there it was. The cheeky smile that would forever and always melt my stupid heart. "I've only been here for like, twenty minutes, and look! You've already gotten to me. I'm losing the plot, and you won't even speak to me, and I mean, I'm only here because I still love you. I mean, what the fuck?"

I just stared at him, not really understanding why he was yelling at me. Nor did I understand a single word of what he just said, spoken in a weird mishmash of English and German.

"We need to talk?" I repeated.

His words were echoing, resonating in my skull. *In love, love you, drama, love you, love, love, love, I love you.* They just didn't make sense, not coming from him, *careful Andreas*, a year older than me, yet we'd always been equals, even when I'd felt younger, more innocent, more curious, less mature and grown up.

I guess that's what you got when you grew up with a dad you silently feared would go full-blown mad every time his moods swung. You got edgy and somewhat nervous, and you felt really crappy about it because he was your dad anyway, the best dad anyone could ask for even in his highest or lowest moments, especially when you had the two best dads in the world. Then your dad got sick and your whole life imploded into some fragile situation where you made rash decisions and things went to shit. Like now.

Andreas had his share too, I knew that. Both Bruno and Gabriel had struggled, but perhaps they'd managed to hide it better from their kids. Andreas and I had had this great deep talk about depression and mania when I was around nineteen, and he'd said that while he knew his dads had suffered a lot, he'd never been afraid, not even worried. He was just sad when people were sad.

I'd been surprised because I'd thought everyone was afraid. I'd always feared that my dad would one day kill himself, ever since I'd come across some medical papers on bipolar when I was around ten years old and home alone. But it was what it was. He was still alive, and I tried not to think about it whenever I thought about him.

My mind seemed to spin sometimes, it blew out thoughts and ideas at high speed but still somehow arranged them in neat little rows. Mostly, I felt connected. I could make a straight line between them, from my fear to the conversations with Andreas in my bed, lying chest to chest with our legs entwined, his mouth a warm breath from my own, a small movement from my lips, his smile, his laughter, the light in his eyes, his eyelids the microsecond before he kissed me...to now, when he was standing here, still angry.

His chest heaved in and out, too fast, too deep. The way he was looking at me, a ridiculous game of *kiss, marry, kill* sprang to mind, spinning me back in time, or perhaps it was in the future, after Andreas, before now, I couldn't remember anymore.

Suddenly the door swung open again, hitting the wall hard, and Andreas jolted forward in surprise, falling face first onto the bed, or rather into my lap.

"Shit. Sorry. You were in the middle of something. We really didn't mean to disturb you!"

The girls were standing in the middle of the room, tipsy and chuckling, their cheeks red, each of them holding a steaming glass mug of highly spiked mulled wine—Thomas's 'seasonal blend', no doubt, with Maria's spice mix and Frank's apple juice from the garden. It was a new interest he'd developed and kept over the past years, hoarding apples in all the neighbouring gardens and making apple juice from them. His brews were quite popular at the local farmer's market, despite my father the farmer living well inside the urban parts of Oslo.

"Are they busy?" Thomas's voice sounded from the hallway outside a moment before he stepped in, holding a glass mug towards us. "We thought you might want some. It's Frank's juice and Maria's spice mix."

As I'd suspected.

"Frank's juice." Bruno chuckled and appeared beside Thomas, his cheeks already deep red. Apparently, he'd had more than one mug of wine already. He'd probably also forgotten to eat again—another of Bruno's silly traits.

"Koffer." Gabriel nudged his husband and laughed. "And there is some pretty good Äpfel Schnapps in it as well." He held up another mug.

"Yes, the idiot wouldn't let me use Amaretto." Bruno giggled, bumping Gabriel with his hip. "Sei proprio scemo, amore mio."

Ten years ago, we would probably have rolled our eyes and found them sickeningly annoying, but these days I understood how deep their continuous love and respect ran, although Gabriel looked a little offended by Frank's suggestion.

"Amaretto in Glühwein? It's bad enough that these Vikings want to use apple juice as a base, but Amaretto? Ugh. And don't think talking Italiano to me will get you laid."

"Do you remember the red juice they called Glühwein the first year we were here?" Both the Germans grimaced.

"That was gløgg," Frank protested. "And yeah, it had nothing to do with glühwein! But this one is the proper shit." He pointed into his cup. "The red one was way too sweet, but this one is perfect. Dry apple juice, some lemon and oranges, spices, and then that Schnapps you so generously brought. Besides, this is what we have here now. You know, embrace your local culture, try new foods and all that?"

"Yeah, yeah." Bruno waved his arms about, spilling wine on the floor. "It's wonderful. I'm just teasing, my Lieblingskoffer."

"Liebling ist okay, aber Koffer? Ich? Der bist ja dann wohl eher du!" They kissed with a loud smacking noise, and Bruno laughed and almost tripped over. Frank barely managed to save their mugs.

Andreas's head was still planted between my legs, and I prayed to an almighty figure I didn't believe in that the shivers I felt between my legs were him laughing and not something else. My face felt cold and stiff, I might as well have been dead and wearing a death mask, except that I still felt like throwing up.

"Dads, I think we should leave. I still think they're doing something here," Maria said, winking at me while trying to herd them all out of my suddenly too crowded bedroom. The wall of chuckling and laughter and loud, drunk voices finally disappeared through the door, leaving only Andreas, me and the deafening vacuum in the room.

For a moment, we both lay there. I honestly couldn't move, and besides, it was a deep-running, comfortable feeling having Andreas across me again. We'd cuddled what felt like all our lives, and feeling his body against mine had once been a habit—a habit we'd turned into something that felt like hate. I slammed my fist into his arm.

He moved slightly before slowly rising off me and the bed, holding his arm and staring at me. "What the fuck?" he mumbled, and I was suddenly, acutely aware that his shaking earlier had definitely not been laughter. His face was painted with tears, and the redness of his eyes was something I couldn't bear. I hated his tears. I hated the pain. I hated...fuck, everything. So did he.

"Fuck, fuck," he whispered before storming out of the room, leaving the door wide open like he'd expected me to follow. I briefly heard the hooting and giggling from the kitchen before someone hushed them; the sounds shut off again as the kitchen door slammed shut.

I went to sleep shortly after, not even bothering to brush my teeth or use the bathroom first, since the bathroom was too close to the kitchen and I absolutely didn't want to see anyone right now. At least I fell asleep fast, and my sleep was apparently deep and good, as I felt weirdly rested when I woke up.

The only problem was visible on my mobile screen, showing that the time was just gone two in the morning and I was now wide awake, not a cell in my body left in sleep mode, despite not having slept more than six hours. I went to the bathroom and brushed my teeth, but the bright light and the icy feeling of mint toothpaste only made me feel even more awake.

For a while, I lay in bed, rolling from side to side, counting sheep, trying to visualise my limp body falling asleep starting from the fingertips, but nothing helped. I tried to wank, since the after-bliss made me sleepy, and it was no joke that men usually fell asleep after sex. Probably women, too, if the orgasm felt the same. If they came, that was. I'd more often than not disappointed in the orgasm department, not quite understanding how to make things right, and gender clearly hadn't been the issue. Humans were strange creatures, and I'd been told more than once that I was an impatient and selfish lover.

Not even getting myself off helped. If anything, I felt even more tense afterwards. I couldn't stop the feelings rushing through my brain and body, his eyes, his soft hair, his warm breath against my crotch today, his arms, stomach, legs, the sounds... Fuck, I was getting hard again.

With a frustrated sigh, I rolled onto my back and put both hands on top of the duvet, fisting the covers while trying to ignore the rhythmic beats between my legs.

After a few minutes I gave up and threw the duvet aside before putting my feet on the ice-cold floor. *The basement must be like a fridge by now.* Heating was expensive, and the basement had always been a cold and unfriendly place in the winter. Hopefully, Andreas had a pile of blankets in addition to the thick duvet down there, but somehow I doubted he'd ask for anything even if he was freezing to death.

I pulled on my joggers and a hoodie and padded out into the small hallway. At the kitchen door, I stopped to listen, but I couldn't hear anything and no light was getting through the narrow openings around Maria's bedroom door upstairs. I held my breath and carefully opened the door to the kitchen, soon enveloped by a comforting darkness and quiet as I tiptoed towards the door to the stairs that led down to the basement, familiar movements I'd made thousands of times.

I felt for the doorframe, but before I found it, the world turned bright around me, and I squeaked, sounding something like a very small, frightened animal, I thought.

"Where are you going?" His voice was raspy behind me, but I could hear the smirk.

"Nowhere," I stuttered out. "I was just—"

"We both know this door only leads to the basement, Freddie."

My shoulders slumped, and I let go of the handle. I sighed, a little too loudly, hoping I didn't look completely dishevelled as I turned around to face him.

"Come sleep in my room," I said. My voice came out as a whisper. I couldn't even talk properly. "Come...please."

The idea of bringing him back to bed was probably one of the worst I'd ever had. I couldn't even begin to describe how dumb I felt asking...no, begging him to come lie with me. No matter what he answered, it was a dangerous thing to do. We shouldn't start this again. We never should have started it in the first place. We should have ended it years ago, just like we had. Yet we stumbled into this dance of deceit, again and again and again.

Without a word, he followed me. I grabbed his hands, and we moved across the kitchen to the hallway where he walked me backwards into my room. His hands were cold in mine, and our nervous breathing and the low squelching of our bare feet against the floor were the only sounds I heard.

He'd already disappeared under the duvet before I had taken off my hoodie, reclaiming his place next to the wall. Once a boy, now a man with messy hair against the pillow, his body curled under the duvet, which he held up for me to get under, next to him, clearly wanting to spoon me. He was always the big spoon first, and only now I realised he'd stripped down to his boxers, his skin ice cold as I placed my palm on his chest.

"It's already half past two. Shouldn't I be the big spoon?" I blurted, far too easily slipping into our old routine. "Besides, you're stone cold. Let me warm you up a bit?" I tried to tangle my legs around his, another instinctive reaction, to get him warm, but he turned me around by the shoulders, putting me exactly where he needed me.

He shook his head, but I heard his smile as he said, "Let's sleep in tomorrow and just stay in bed all day. Then you can do all the spooning you want."

"Okay."

It's funny how I didn't question his suggestion, just accepting it as normal. I fell asleep without a second's thought, with his breath on my neck and his hand in mine.

At ten, I woke up with my arms around him. His fingers were still entwined with mine, his thumb moving in slow, lazy circles across the back of my hand. I curled closer around him and pulled the duvet over our shoulders. His hair tickled my cheek when I kissed his neck.

"I missed you," I whispered.

His words were muffled against the pillow, but I still made them out—those two words that stabbed me in the heart. "Me too," he said. "Me too."

Chapter Five
Andreas

"This is so fucked up," I muttered, mostly to myself, to try to calm the panic rising in my chest. I was still stroking his hand, almost like a nervous tic. We shouldn't be doing this. What the hell was I thinking? Wandering around the empty house like a zombie in the middle of the night because I couldn't sleep. I'd even tidied up the kitchen, watered the plants and the massive amaryllis bulbs, and collected mugs and glasses from everywhere, tiptoeing around like some half-naked waiter, balancing a tray of dirty stuff I had found in the bathroom. The girls had all gone out to some club then come back, waking me up with the clatter of glasses and too-loud giggling before disappearing off upstairs, the house falling silent almost as soon as their door shut.

"I know," he replied, his voice barely there. "I don't know what we're doing. I don't know what I'm supposed to say."

"You broke up with me. You tell me." I was back to being pissed off. Again.

"We were never together in the first place." He was talking too fast. "I wanted to be. I wanted us to try, and you couldn't even say it out loud. Then you come back here, seven years later, and shout that you love me? Fuck off, Andreas."

He pushed me away and rolled over on his side, away from me. My back instantly felt cold and damp from the loss of his body. I shuddered,

I couldn't help it, and curled into a ball like I was trying to protect myself from the inevitable backlash, stop all my truths coming out of my mouth.

"You didn't want what I wanted," he continued quietly. "And anyway, you kept saying that you weren't gay and that you just wanted to be—what was it again? *Nothing like my parents.*"

He was dishing out the words like they were poison, and every syllable was meant to hurt. Trust me, they did. Daggers to my soul, every single one.

"Freddie, I had a massive breakdown after we broke up. I couldn't get out of bed for weeks. You didn't even care. I begged you to come to me, and you wouldn't."

"I was still at uni, 'Dreas. How was I supposed to just bugger off to Berlin like that? You kept saying that we were nothing. Friends. Just friends. Funny, that, when we were fucking like rabbits."

I didn't know how to respond to that even though I knew he was right. But that had been years ago. I still suffered with weeks when I couldn't get out of bed. I still questioned fucking everything. And he was absolutely right. I still couldn't say things out loud.

"I'm sorry," I said instead and rolled onto my back so that we were lying there, shoulder to shoulder, both of us staring at the ceiling in silence.

After a while, he said, "We need to talk. You're right about that. But I can't hook up with you again and have you ignore me for the next six months. I can't do casual. Not with you."

"We didn't hook up," I snarled. I didn't know why I was so angry when he'd done exactly what I'd wanted him to do. I'd wandered around the house clattering glasses for an hour hoping to wake him up so he would come and get me and tuck me into his bed. I couldn't even deny that that had been my plan. "If we're going to do this, we need to be honest. Spill the fucking truth," I told the ceiling.

"Okay?" He let out a deep breath. "You're an arsehole."

"Thank you for sharing," I hissed, but I was smiling. "My turn?"

"Be my guest!"

"Okay. Er..." It was harder than I'd thought, finding the right words for all the things I'd wanted to tell him over the years. "There have been moments over the last couple of years when stuff's happened, and the first thing I have thought of is you. Almost like for a minute I forget all of this ever went down. Thinking that you would have laughed. I wanted to text you and send you pictures—the number of times I almost rang you but then

I chickened out..." I had to stop to catch my breath. My heart was beating a little too fast for my liking.

"You were never brave enough," he said, finishing my sentence. He knew me so well, even after seven years of radio silence.

"I am still a chicken. I bail out as soon as things get serious," I admitted. I was trying, really trying here. There were things that needed to be said, but honesty had never been my forte.

"Have you... I mean, I speak to Lilly a lot, so she gives me most of the gossip, but, has there been anyone? Anyone serious?"

I smiled at the twang of jealousy that was an unmistakable feature in his voice. Just that little edge. It was still there, and somehow, I liked that.

"I have hooked up with girls. Had a few flings but nothing else. It's just, you know. I tried...with men, at clubs." Who was I kidding here? The truth was that honesty was fucking brutal. I tried not to even analyse this shit for myself, and here I was trying to explain it, to Freddie of all people.

"Hate clubs," he said. "Like a meat market. Never did well with Grindr either."

"But you had boyfriends?"

"Sure, I had a couple. Great guys. I'm still in contact with Eric— he's getting married in February. Retreat in Wisconsin. Nice couple."

Now it was me behaving like a green-eyed monster, hissing under my breath, "I couldn't do other guys. They did absolutely nothing for me. Not a twitch. Couldn't get it up, not even when I was drunk and some really hot guy tried to blow me in the bathroom. It was...humiliating at best. I'm not gay, Freddie. I am really, *really* sure of that."

"Has it completely escaped your messed-up brain that I made you come, without even touching you, several times, while my dick was up your arse? I think that counts as super gay. Very fucking super gay." Now he was fuming too, and I didn't blame him. I would be pissed off with me as well.

"I didn't say straight, did I?" I hurled back at him. "I just don't fancy other blokes. I tried, okay? I met up with this couple, this girl who wanted to see her boyfriend fuck another bloke because the idea of that turned her on no end, and he was really fit, and she was fucking beautiful. It was the filthiest fucking fantasy I could imagine, getting off with the two of them."

"Threesomes are fucked up," he said casually. How was he so fucking calm when I was sprouting a headache with all this talking? All this emotion. And I still hadn't told him anything of substance.

"I'm fucking this up. Just look at me. I walked around the house last night..." I sat up and shuffled around, trying to find a comfortable position where I didn't feel so raw, dragged the duvet up over my shoulders once I'd finally settled down. Despite the room being warm, I had chills and goosebumps everywhere. "I hoped you would wake up and come and drag me into your bed. This is my happy place. *You* are my happy place."

Okay. Now I sounded like that teenaged lovesick idiot from my youth.

"You told me to be honest. Then fucking be honest with me back. What the hell do you want, Andreas?"

Now he sat up and snagged his hoodie off the floor, dragging it over his head, which gave me a few seconds to admire his naked chest. Because, well. It was right there, and Freddie, who had always been that skinny kid with ribs everywhere, was now built and buff and my mouth was watering. He was stunning. He was a man, obviously, and here I was with a drool pool in my mouth.

"I want to be happy, and I want to have you in my life, however I can," I admitted, sounding broken and pathetic, and here came the tears. Fucking hell. Twenty-seven years old and crying in my ex-boyfriend's bed. What a loser.

"It's been years," he said quietly. "You fucked off out my life and ignored me. I tried to text. I rang you."

"You broke up with me," I slobbered, hiding my eyes behind the edge of the duvet.

"I gave you the choice. Either you were my boyfriend and we were together and you made an effort—"

"Or I could fuck right off," I interrupted. "I remember that conversation. Kind of hard to forget having someone crush you like that."

"*You* fucking crushed me. All I wanted was for you to say *I love you*. You couldn't even do that."

And, of course, that was the moment when I snorted, trying to regain my composure, and Lilly kicked the door open, carrying two cups of coffee in her outstretched hands.

"Oh, darling Fredrik, now you've made Andreas cry. Cheer up, brother dearest, here is your morning coffee. All is well, and it's Christmas," she sang out far too cheerily. Her eyeliner was smudged under her eyes, and there was a piece of purple tinsel stuck in her fringe. I meant to point this out to her, but I didn't dare to speak because then I would properly start to cry.

"Good night, Lils?" Freddie asked like there was nothing wrong in the world.

"It was awesome!" My little sister giggled and crawled onto his lap like she was ten years old all over again. "Maria took us to this gay club, and we danced until it closed, and then we went to some underground bar that her boyfriend knew of, with podium dancers, and we had shots, and have you met Maria's friend Sverre? Such a nice guy! I need to meet a Norwegian guy, someone with loads of money, because now I'm skint. We had kebabs on the way home, and then Lotts threw up in a pile of snow. I've never laughed so much. Anyway, Uncle Frank is baking..."

"Breathe, Lils," Freddie said calmly and stroked her head. "Breathe."

I needed to have words with my sister about her inappropriate affection for Freddie. She wasn't a child anymore, and he...I couldn't say it. What the hell was wrong with me?

"Frank is baking," she repeated and took a gulp of coffee out of Freddie's cup. "Vati and Papi are out shovelling snow, and Thomas is going out to pick up some top-secret Christmas present so I need to get ready because I'm going with him. Lotts is fast asleep—can you check on her and Maria later? Just to make sure they are still breathing? God, I love Christmas here. Have you seen the snow? There was at least two feet of fresh snow last night. Loads. Everywhere." She took another deep breath, and I couldn't help smiling at her as she clambered off the bed in her brushed-cotton pyjamas. "I'm off. Just wanted to make sure the two of you hadn't killed each other. We all laughed when your bed downstairs was empty this morning, 'Dreas. Like we didn't know where you'd be."

She twirled out the door, blowing us kisses as she disappeared, of course leaving the door wide open. I could hear Uncle Frank in the kitchen, whistling along to the Christmas music blasting from the speakers, the scent of baking unmistakable in the air.

"What happened with this threesome then?" Freddie asked.

I turned to look at him, taking in the little smirk at his question, the lashes framing his eyes, the way his lips closed around the rim of the coffee cup, the slight tremble in his hand.

"Don't want to talk about it," I muttered.

"We do need to talk about stuff," he insisted. "You said we should be honest, and if we're to have any chance of surviving this holiday, you have to talk to me. Properly."

I felt sick. "You broke up with me, and it messed me up to the point where I lost the plot."

"Then we went to that freaky castle in France."

I swallowed hard. "You wouldn't speak to me. You barely said goodbye when we went home that summer." I was trying to keep it civil. I was trying to be calm.

"You wouldn't *let* me speak to you."

"I hated you. I hated everything."

"You broke me. And what the hell did you do to make it better?" He kept his voice low, but I could tell he wanted to shout. "You brought a girl on our holiday and went on some fucking rebound right in front of my fucking face. She thought she was your girlfriend! What the fuck, 'Dreas? Where was your head? What were you thinking?"

"Nothing," I said, trying to keep my voice stable. "It was all for you. Fuck, it was always about you."

Chapter Six
Fredrik

THINGS GOT KIND of foggy after that. We shouted hurtful truths and hurled insults at each other, like nothing had actually ever changed. Then he stormed off, same as always, slamming the door like a temperamental teen while I roared into the silence he'd left behind.

It was the week before Christmas, my entire family were tiptoeing around on tenterhooks, and it was all my fault. Well, half my fault. I wasn't going to carry the entire burden of this, not when the dickhead across the room was acting like he was some kind of saint.

He wasn't. He was mean and cruel and immature and...I didn't know how to deal with him. So I slipped back into being the old me and chose to ignore him, sat at the kitchen table and put my head on Lilly's shoulder. She didn't even question if I was okay. Everyone knew I wasn't. We were back to being a house of unspoken truths, hiding behind the shiny surface lie of celebrating Christmas.

I hadn't come back home to celebrate anything. I'd come back home because I'd had no choice. My life had once again been irrevocably turned upside down, and here I was, cursing the world for its cruelty. Because life wasn't good. It never would be, ever again, as we all sat in silence listening to Frank throwing up in the bathroom next door, Thomas's muffled voice coming through in between the retching.

Everyone was acting weird, trying to rush into stupid traditions that meant shit. The girls had gone ice skating because we *always* went ice skating, like we always baked all this stuff that nobody ever ate. Then Thomas chucked it in the bin in January, cursing the food waste and money spent that he was now throwing straight into landfill. Maria would kill us all if she knew.

I sat at the breakfast table, eating one festive treat after another like a robot, not knowing what else to do because doing anything else or opening my mouth to speak was painful and awkward. I couldn't find a comfortable space to exist, and it was doing my head in. Andreas, apparently, had no such problem, discussing world politics with my sister like he was some kind of expert. He wasn't. He was full of shit and he knew it. He briefly glanced over to meet my eye, but I looked away. I didn't know what else I was supposed to do.

I homed in on the giant casserole dish on the stove, hoping to nab that job for the morning. It would give me an excuse to bow out of the festive traditions that would require me to smile when there was nothing left to smile about.

Luckily for me, everyone seemed to effortlessly disappear, leaving me to clear the table and keep my head busy with chores. I loaded the dishwasher and wiped down surfaces, simple actions that left nothing but shine behind, then gathered bags of flour, baking sheets scratched and scorched with memories from years of use, and a giant brown slab of gingerbread dough that had been resting outside overnight. Frank must have brought it in in the early hours of the morning, as it was frozen solid, and when I tipped it out on the table, it was like dropping a brick. The table's legs creaked alarmingly against the floorboards. It would take some effort, some elbow grease and maybe a bit of violence to turn the lump of sugar, butter and syrupy spices into something pliable enough to mould with my feeble fingers, but I needed it. I needed something to take the edge off all the anger inside me, all the things I couldn't control.

I needed to sit down and make some kind of plan, but even that seemed too complicated in my head, so I kept on bashing the dough against the table, filling the air with thumps and flour and my senses with scents that reminded me of childhood, of times when my head hadn't been such a frightening space.

I wasn't depressed. The world was just fucked up, and I'd never been equipped to handle it. I was no better than Andreas because we were both the same. Things got hard, and we ran—in opposite directions, it seemed—

and I was starting to realise that I was just as much of the arsehole here. I'd run away when I should have sat him down, except I had tried to talk to him, and what had he done? He'd run away. Sighing, I dropped the dough brick and ripped my hoodie over my head, leaving me just in a T-shirt and pyjama bottoms. We didn't dress up for Christmas here. This was a family affair, yet I felt bewildered and lonely, awfully so, and I again hated that it wasn't just the four of us. All I wanted right now was comfort and reassurance that we would make it through the next year in one piece.

The truth was something I'd hidden way, way back in my brain, the sole reason I'd packed up my life and returned home with no plan and no backup. I wanted to be here, *needed* to be here, spending my time with the people who mattered instead of bouncing around in the company of strangers, people who never would matter.

"Hey." Here he was. Dickhead of the century. I'd honestly thought he'd left with the others, but he was freshly showered and looked as nervous as I was. He did that to me. Made me all jittery. Even doing a simple thing like washing his hands in the sink and tying Frank's threadbare apron around his waist had me taking small shallow breaths as I wrung my hands and hoped he would just go away.

"I'm not going away," he said like he knew every single thought in my head, and he meant it too, as he sat at the table and stuck his hand in the bag of flour. "I checked on Frank. He's having a nap. Took his vitals and filled in the form on the side."

"Not your job," I pointed out grumpily. "The nurses come twice a day. Thomas does the rest."

"He's okay."

"I know he's okay."

"Thomas is sorting out the last of the shopping and driving the girls around like some taxi service."

"As he does every year. And there's still a shitload of work to be done."

"Freddie, sometimes I think you forget that I'm a proper nurse. Under all this bullshit, I do have some hardcore training, enough to read between the lines of what's happening here. It's hard to ignore the massive amount of medication stashed on the worktop over there. Don't pretend you don't know. Don't pretend that I don't know."

"I don't want to talk about it."

"I know you don't."

We were as prickly as each other, hurling short, sharp sentences around like angry fireflies. And just like that, my shoulders slumped and my head fell into my hands, and I stood there in my own kitchen with the smell of happiness and laughter on my fingertips and tried my hardest not to burst into tears.

"Can we just...not?" was all I managed to say.

"Oh, Freddie."

I leant on the tabletop, my arms taking all my weight, and Andreas...

Andreas just ripped that dough brick in half as if it was nothing and started working on the piece in front of him. Strong, steady movements, kneading and pushing, his breathing calm and easy next to my own ragged breaths.

"Do you remember the first time we met?" he asked, dropping in a little smile. I stared at him; I couldn't help it. "So, we were, like total strangers, and we didn't even speak the same language. Well, we both spoke English, but I wasn't comfortable speaking it out loud, and neither were you. But we kind of got our phones out, and you were showing me something, and I pulled up screenshots of messages from my Twitch channel or whatever, and you laughed at me. I think you called me a show-off. Teased me about having a load of followers who sent me love hearts in the chat section."

"You were freaking proud of it," I huffed out, but I was smiling too. I'd forgotten he had that effect on me. He soothed my bleeding wounds, made the dark world around me a little brighter.

"I was. You have no idea how much I was into all that crap. Thought my world revolved around subs and stats and likes and fucking twinkling stardom, which in the end meant shit. My channel died a dire death. Killed it off that year when I couldn't...you know. What I'm trying to say, Freddie, is that you calm me. I just need to sit here and you calm me. You always did, and I don't bloody know how you do it. Witchcraft, I tell you."

I laughed. It seemed a strange thing to do in the circumstances. "You've been the centre of my world ever since that day, although I don't think I realised how besotted I was with you until that stupid camping trip."

"You still thought you were straight," he said with a wink.

"Don't!" I warned. We'd been here before, and it was not a discussion I was willing to have again. It never ended well.

"Freddie." He knotted his fingers into a fist and gave the dough a heavy thwack before folding his arms and treating me to that intense stare that frightened the living daylights out of me—only because of how it made me feel. He was too close. Too much. Too everything when my brittle head couldn't even deal with myself.

"Life is right here, Freddie. Not yesterday or ten years ago. Not that summer in France and not that ski trip, or the many summers we spent at Bella's. That is not life, or not my life, anyway. My life is right here, and I still don't know how to live it. I didn't want to come here, I'll happily admit that, and that's me being absolutely honest. I was terrified of coming here because I didn't want to do this. Didn't want to face up to all these truths."

"None of us want to face up to this," I hissed. I'd told him I didn't want to talk about it, and here he was, sticking his nose into stuff that wasn't his to deal with.

"You guys are my family. Don't shut us out of this like we don't know what you're going through. We do because we're right here going through it too."

"And there's nothing we can do to stop it."

"No," he said weakly. "There's nothing we can do to stop it, but I'm right here. I will always be here, and there's nothing we can do to stop that either. I'm right here, Freddie. And you are right there. And this is life. *Our* life."

"There is nothing here that is ours," I snapped, which, sadly, wasn't true. *Everything* in this house was his and mine. All the air, the sky, the woods outside the windows. Everything carried some kind of messed-up Fredrik and Andreas stamp on it, and it was driving me mad, like he was a curse I'd never be free of.

"I love you," he said, and for the first time ever those words made me choke on my breath. I sat down on the chair that was thankfully still behind me or I would have fallen flat on the floor. I couldn't look at him, though, and instead stared at my flour-covered hands.

"I'll say it again because I know you don't believe me, since we've barely even spoken in the past seven years, but it's still there. Always will be. You're sat there with flour in your hair, and there's a bit of dough on your cheek, and I know you don't feel the same way about me anymore, and that's fine. I just want you to know that I still love you. I always have, since that first moment we sat next to each other. I loved you when we went on that crazy moose safari and you held my hand. I loved you when we went shopping and then I threw up in that field and you rubbed my back. I slept on your lap in the car, remember?"

All distant, stupid memories from years and years ago, things I shouldn't remember, but I did. I remembered the smell. The taste of pizza. The wind in my hair. The sight of his stupid cheap aftershave that he'd left behind. I still had the empty can under my bed—something else I'd never tell him.

"That was the first time you slept in my bed," I said.

"And I pretended to fall asleep because I didn't want to leave. You made me happy. You still do."

"Even when I shout at you?"

"Yup. Even when you shout at me."

It was strange how I was now totally calm, how everything was falling back into place, back to the way we'd once been, when words hadn't meant broken hearts and we'd yet to figure out all those truths. When life had truly been right there in the moment and not lived through memories that I wanted to forget more than anything.

"Let's not talk about it," he said, surprising me with his sudden sensibility. "Let's just bake, put some sounds on and let things be. We need to do this Christmas thing right, and anyway, I promised Frank I'd make a whole tray of those stupid unicorn-shaped cookies."

"I hate that cutter. Bloody useless."

He smiled. Shook his head. Smiled again.

"We can do this, Freddie. Just live in the now with me for a bit. Don't think too hard."

"You sound like Frank, dumbass."

"Frank is a very wise man."

I slammed my fist into the piece of dough in front of me...and gratefully accepted the rolling pin Andreas held out for me.

"Roll and bake," he instructed, quietly grabbing a baking tray from inside the oven.

"Roll and bake," I repeated, pressing the wooden pin into the dough. It barely made a dent. "No thinking."

"No thinking."

Chapter Seven
Andreas

It was easier said than done, but we somehow muddled through it with the help of Celine Dion wailing out festive favourites on Spotify. Then we did Mariah Carey, then the endless Christmas mix tapes from our youth, the same songs on repeat, the way we always had. And yes, it was safe and comforting and we had a great system going, filling our trays with finely cut shapes, every cutter making us laugh, telling stories we already knew, remembering where certain cutters had been bought and when they had been added to Frank's never-ending collection of cookie cutters. Freddie had bought loads of new ones in the States, and Vati and I had made it a yearly competition to see how many new ones we could sneak in without Frank noticing. He always did. He always found them and called us out on them and made us use them. We made far too many gingerbread biscuits, and when the girls came home, I backed off, letting them take over. It was too much noise for my fragile head to cope with and I needed a breather, a place where I could just let myself think.

I retreated into the quiet bedroom at the far end of the living room. It had once been some kind of library but was now Frank and Thomas's bedroom. An arrangement that worked far better than the loft area where they'd always slept before. *Before* was the loaded word, and I could no longer remember how I'd found out. Just a whispered unease, words unspoken and a grief that my Vati had carried on his shoulders over the last year. However much Frank was trying to mask it, we all knew he wasn't going to win this fight, and what should be a bedroom looked like a hospital suite. There was too much equipment for my liking, too many smells that took me back to places I really didn't want to go.

"This is not your job," Frank said sternly as I once again tightened the blood pressure cuff around his arm—an arm that had previously held shapely muscle but now looked disturbingly thin.

"I know," I said softly. "Occupational hazard."

"Idiot." Frank smiled. "At least you're nicer than those temp nurses that are covering over Christmas. All my usual people are on holiday, and the one who came last night was a right bitch."

"Don't say that. They're just not used to you. Not like us."

"You guys are my family. The nurses are a pain. A necessary one, but still a pain."

"Of course they are, but you're doing good, Frank."

"I was fine yesterday, and now today I can't get out of bed. Told you. Everything is a pain."

He sighed, and his body shifted in the bed as he struggled to sit up. I sighed too because he was too pig-headed to ask for help. Instead, I took his hand, using those well-practised manoeuvres to place him into a more comfortable position, then pushed the pillows behind his back, got his duvet tucked in under his chin and chuckled when he gave me that look of evil.

"Do you know how many times I've lain in this bed wishing my life away?"

"Lows do that to you, Uncle Frank." I wasn't mocking him. I knew what he was saying.

"And now I'm stuck here like a cripple, and my body is doing exactly what I asked. Killing me slowly and painfully, and there is nothing I can do to stop it."

He wasn't being morbid, just telling it like it was. Frank had never minced his words, and for once I was relieved he was talking to me. Straight up. Not that I didn't know.

"Not your fault. You didn't bring this on yourself, if that's what you're suggesting." I made myself comfortable on the bed next to him. "This? This is life at its cruellest. We just have to take it and make it something we can deal with."

"Thomas is dealing with it better than anyone. Maria too." He said it without saying the words: *Freddie isn't dealing with anything.*

There was no easy solution to this. I hadn't come here for the happily ever after. I'd come here because as a family, blood or not, we'd had no choice. We all needed to be here.

"You've said it yourself, many times," I started, wringing my hands. "Life is not the future. Not the past. Life is what is right in front of us, and we just have to take it for what it is."

"Wise words, kiddo." Frank chuckled. "And you should take heed. Both of you, or I might have to side with Maria and start calling you Idiot One and Idiot Two. Both of you live in a past full of mistakes and arguments and broken hearts. Yet here you are."

"Here we are," I agreed.

"Took me long enough, but the last couple of years have been perfect. Things have been good. My life has been so wonderful. Thomas and I... we've had the best life. Some really good times. We did things, some insane things. Travelled, and worked and got..." He stopped and smiled.

"You have indeed. Your life has been kind of brilliant."

"I don't want it to stop. I want to fight. I will fight this with every last breath in this knackered old body of mine. For Thomas. For Maria and Fredrik. For you guys. I have to because what else can I do?"

"That's good. And we will fight with you, you know that."

"I don't want to leave. I don't want to lose everything I have. There's nothing on the other side. I don't believe in anything like that. I just want everything to be good. For everyone else. Things need to be taken care of." He was tired again, closing his eyes.

"Tomorrow will be a good day," I told him.

"The day before yesterday was such a good day. I had so much energy."

"And today you have less. Tomorrow you'll have more."

"I always loved Christmas. The snow, the lights, the smell in the air."

"Want to go outside tomorrow? Just sit on the veranda and have coffee? We do that at Christmas, remember? I'll even get the girls to have a snowball fight for you."

He chest moved up and down with small bouts of silent laughter. "Snowball fights. Those girls always loved a good snowball fight. Remember when Lotts climbed a tree with a bucket of snowballs and got me real good? I never even saw that attack coming."

"Was that the year Papi fell over and sprained his wrist? He thought his career as a surgeon was over. Nightmare. Remember him whining all New Year's Day?"

"Every year he falls over at some point. God knows how he walks a straight line, that man."

"Or not such a straight line." I giggled. It was a stupid joke, but Frank loved a stupid joke. So did Freddie.

"I've got Freddie," I said quietly. "He will always have me, and I will always look after him, try to make him happy. I've been rubbish at it lately, but you know I will." I couldn't be sure what I was promising, but I wanted him to know, and I wanted so badly for my words to be true.

He nodded. "Just remember there's no heaven out there. Heaven is what we make right here on Earth. The people we make happy. The laughter. Hugs. All the bloody hugs. Remember that, kiddo. Make it count. Every freaking second. And don't lie in bed and dwell on shit that means nothing. Because life is right here, right under your nose. Go live it. You know it makes sense."

I smiled. "You sound like me."

"I do, don't I? Now let me sleep, and tomorrow morning, I expect you up and helping me make bread. It's Christmas. We need bread."

"We bloody do," I said. "Go to sleep. I'll keep an eye on things until Thomas is back."

He didn't reply, just smiled as he rolled over and fell asleep. I sat there for a while, listening to him breathing. He wasn't going anywhere. Not yet. He wasn't meant to go at all because he had a whole life left to live. We all did.

None of us were ready to go anywhere, least of all myself.

****

The evening was actually pleasant after that. Dinner was made, and we all filled our plates and gathered in the bedroom, most of us sitting on the floor as Frank held court in bed and called us all uncivilised heathens. Vati had all the candles burning in the windows, and the sounds from the TV in the living room made the mood almost normal. There were giggles and laughter and Thomas and Papi telling stories and the girls sharing more than probably needed sharing. It felt good. It almost felt like happiness— a happiness my head tried to tell me I didn't deserve.

I retreated back down to the basement, leaving Vati laying the table for breakfast and Maria buzzing around trying to find a place to hide the last of her gifts. Freddie had disappeared, and I was once again exhausted from trying to keep everything together. My head. My sanity. My brittle heart. I may have been all cocky and confident on the outside, but on the inside

I was slowly crumbling. The hot shower I took hurt my skin, and my clothes felt wrong on my body. I didn't know what to do with myself.

Well, I did, because I let my feet take me back upstairs, to the quiet hallway where my Papi was stood scratching his stubbled chin.

"Papi," I greeted with a polite nod.

"Dreas," he responded with an evil grin.

"Oh, stop it." I sighed.

"Sit down for a sec." He motioned to the stairs.

I knew better than to argue. There was some kind of telling-off coming. I may have been twenty-seven, but I would always be my Papi's child, and he was speaking Italian, which always meant trouble.

So I dealt with it the only way I could. Truths.

"Papi," I started, plonking myself down on the step next to him.

"'Dreas."

"Papi, I love Freddie."

He didn't smile. He right out loud chuckled. "Is this what I think it is? Is this you finally coming out to me? At the tender age of twenty-seven?"

He was taking the piss when I wasn't.

"Don't mock me."

"I'm not mocking you, son. I've known you were queer since you were very, very young."

"Papi!" Now I was shrieking, waving my hands around in sheer frustration. "You have zero gaydar, zero clue. What the hell are you talking about?"

"Oh, come on, son. Andreas Moretti-Fischer. Gorgeous, beautiful boy. You have always loved the boys. I mean, even when you had girlfriends, and bless them, poor girls, your heart was never in it. But remember Elis? That boy in your class?"

I grunted. Yeah. He moved away. Broke my fucking heart.

"Then there was that boy Uwe. You were so obsessed with him that his mother rang and asked you to leave him alone. And then Cemil. You loved him. Couldn't stop talking about him."

"Cemil." I sighed. But yeah. I had to reluctantly agree. I'd always had weird fast and crushing friendships. None of them had lasted, but they had burnt strong and bright. Then I'd met Freddie. The one who'd shone the brightest—and still did. Just the mention of his name made my chest hurt.

"And then Fredrik. You fell hard and fast there. Even before that dreaded camping trip, you were besotted. You didn't see it yourself, but the rest of the world did."

Trust my Papi to speak the truth. He always had. I was just not very good at listening.

"I see," I said.

"I know you love him," Papi said quietly. "But thank you for finally trusting me. And whatever you decide to do, Vati and I have your back. Because Fredrik needs you, and if you decide—"

"The truth is, Papi," I interrupted, my body bubbling with irrational frustration. "I...I grew up with all of this...queerness shoved in my face. And I hated it. I don't really understand why, but I was *that* kid. And I didn't want to be like you. I mean, no offence, Papi..."

Yeah, now my Papi was howling.

"You, my darling boy, are exactly like me."

"I know, and I never wanted to be. I didn't want to make the same mistakes, and I didn't want to go through all that you went through. I just wanted to go out there and be...someone else. Someone not so fucked in the head. Again, no offence."

"No offence." My Papi chuckled. "But I don't think anyone here is fucked in the head. We just fall in love, and there's no force in the world that can stop us once we do."

"Doesn't make me gay, though." I sighed.

"No. It doesn't. It makes you human. You connect with people and you give them your whole heart. And when you don't get theirs back? Rejection crushes you into dust. It's not hard to understand where your head has sometimes been at. But lately, I've wondered what you've been thinking. We probably need to have a discussion about some of the things you've done in the past and figure out how to truly learn from our mistakes because you need to make plans for the future now. Real plans. No more messing about."

"What?" That was another stab to my heart. Once again, my parents were one step ahead of me, and...well...the thought had crossed my mind.

"Papi," I whined, then crossed my arms and kind of, weirdly pulled myself together. "Papi, the thing is...I'm really bad at being an adult. I always have been. I can never make decisions. I'm easily led. My confidence is shit at the best of times, and I have no idea how to actually...have a relationship with anyone. But with Freddie... When we first met, he, he kind of got how

I functioned. He understood all of that, even though we were just kids, and he didn't take control or make decisions. He just kind of...led the way, made me see things differently. It was fucking amazing, having someone who saw *me*, and he kept telling me that it was okay to be like me. That I was okay just the way I was. He knew what I needed when I didn't even know it myself. Then when my life went to shit, he wasn't there anymore, and I had no idea how to... All this makes no sense, but now we're here again, and he's right there, in my head. He makes everything calm. Suddenly my head makes sense again."

I had to stop and breathe because my thoughts were all over the place, whirring too fast for me to function.

"I need to be with Freddie. I need him where I am, and I don't know where to start to make plans about that."

I blew out a shaky breath. For the first time in my life, I knew what I needed to make happen, but not how. It felt monumental, but my Papi just scratched his chin and shook his head at me.

"And once again, you're making things complicated when they're not because you know what you need to do. Frank is stable. The chemo is extremely hard on his body, but there's no way of telling if it's turning a corner or killing him. Patience and time. That is all we have on our side now."

"His vitals are good, but his body is worn out. It worries me." It was a relief to change the subject. To give me a moment.

"It worries us all. But you and I are medical professionals, and we look at these things a little differently. Let what we know override our hearts. I still have hope, and that is a dangerous thing. I try to let the statistics speak, the numbers on his journals in there. I read through them with him, and Frank knows what's what. In black and white. I have hope, but I don't dare speak the words."

"Makes me wish we were religious so we could ask that big dude in the sky for some help. Or whoever makes the rules."

"Doesn't hurt to ask. If it makes you feel better."

"Papi?"

"Yeah?"

"Man to Man."

He laughed. My brilliant, kind Papi laughed.

"What do I do with Freddie?"

"Oh, child, that's the easy part. You love him. Whatever happens, you just don't stop loving him. And when things get hard, you love him even more. Unless he breaks your heart, but I doubt he ever will. Because he loves you right back, and you know it."

I wanted so badly to hug him, to cry into his shoulder as I'd done so many times as a child, but my brittle heart was once again threatening to shatter in my chest, so I just squeezed his knee, stood up and walked away. I'd cried too many tears already, and there was a bucket of them in my head ready to spill. I didn't want to cry. I wanted the hurt to end. I wanted my longing to stop. I wanted and needed and all those things suddenly didn't seem so damn complicated, like all the cogs in my head were suddenly aligning. The fucking universe. It had mocked me all my life, and I was sick of it.

The door to Freddie's room was ajar, and I could see him lying there, duvet up to his chin, the light from his phone illuminating his face, brows tightly knitted as he concentrated on whatever he was reading on the screen. He didn't even look up as I walked through the door, closing it quietly behind me.

"And here you are," he said softly.

"Like you knew I would be."

We sounded like a bad pop song from our youth—or an even worse one from the present.

I sat on the bed, folding my too-long legs underneath me as he moved to accommodate me on the mattress. Me and him. He put his phone down, encasing us in darkness, and I traced his face, stroked his hair, out of pure instinct. I did as Frank said. I took my own damn advice and stopped thinking, concentrated on being right here and now with Freddie, rubbed his shoulders, ran my hand down his back, moved the duvet out of the way so I could touch all those familiar curves of his body, relish the comfort of his skin under my fingertips alongside the soundtrack of our breathing. It was nerve-wracking, but I needed this so badly that I didn't know what else to do. Needed him. Needed everything to fall back into place.

My heart beat out of my chest as he grabbed my arm and pulled me close, tucked me under the duvet, my body flush against his. His lips gently pressed to my forehead as our legs tangled until we were simply one body in the bed. Just like we always had been.

Chapter Eight
Fredrik

I COULDN'T EVEN tell who kissed who first, or who took the initiative to start taking off our clothes. My mind went blank with his body all over mine. Or perhaps I was all over him. All I knew was that it was what I wanted and needed, and if things got out of hand...well, my common sense was apparently still somewhere across the Atlantic because it surely wasn't where it was supposed to be. At least one of us had had the presence of mind to get up and actually lock the door, although anyone passing within a metre of the room would have run away anyway. Hopefully. Except if it was one of our sisters, who were nosy as fuck and would have no doubt stood outside and definitely listened in.

He talked a load of crap, whispered needs in my ear, and I whispered them back as underwear got shoved down and dicks were smothered in mouths and tongues, tasting all the pleasures I had so sorely missed. His mouth was a menace, and I craved more. The part about me being a selfish lover was true, always had been. I pushed his head down and fucked his mouth, forcing myself all the way down his throat. I knew he could take it. It wasn't a case of asking permission or consent; this was the way things were with us. I took control because Andreas gave it to me. We'd always rolled like that. He let me explore, try new things—he'd more than willingly let me fuck him that first time. So many years ago. So many memories later.

My dick exploded inside of him, and he gently continued sucking then released me with an embarrassed cough. I wiped tears from under his eyes, kissed his ruined mouth while I jerked him off, small soft movements eliciting all those little sounds I loved. Where I was a selfish dick, he was a needy, gorgeous man, grateful for every gesture, every kiss making him press his body closer to mine. When he finally let go, it was in sheer desperation, and he cried against my chest as I held him as tightly as I could.

I couldn't remember all the words I whispered to him to bring him back down to Earth again, the promises I'd made, the feelings too strong to contain. I was a true Scandinavian man, hiding everything on the inside, a strong armour of control shielding me from the outside. Yet Andreas had always split me wide open, even when he tried not to.

He fell asleep in a snot-and-tear-filled heap of exhaustion, and for once I slept solidly, not a dream in sight. When I woke up, my arms were aching and tingling because he was right where I'd left him, both of us drenched in sweat and our muscles sore. More than a little embarrassment crept in as we detangled ourselves back into reality.

At least my bed linen was already officially soiled with coffee, seeing as it was now covered with more bodily fluids than anyone needed to be made aware of. I bundled it up by habit, thinking I'd take it to the bathroom, then remembered I was back home and the laundry room was downstairs, which meant passing the kitchen and everyone else in the house to reach it.

I shoved the bundle at Andreas. "Can you bring this down to the laundry room?"

He lifted his eyebrow at me. "You're twelve or whatever again and want to get rid of it without your parents seeing?"

"Yes. And so do you. So just throw it in the washer, will you?"

"Now?" he asked, looking down at his naked self with questionable dry, white spots over his defined yet soft stomach, nothing like it had been seven years ago when he'd been a muscular, sporty kid rather than the beautiful man he was today.

"No." I leant in to touch him again, slid my hands down his back, counting his vertebrae under my fingertips on the way to his crack. "Not now."

"What's happening now then?" he teased, dropping the bundle of sheets on the floor.

I didn't answer, just quietly opened my bedroom door and surveyed the sounds from the kitchen. Declaring it safe, I pushed him across the hallway into the bathroom.

Habits were hard to break, and smashing him against the mirrored cabinet created more noise than I had anticipated, but nothing was going to stop me now, not when he was willingly playing along, even though I was questioning the stupidity of my actions myself. But no. It wasn't stupid. It was who we were and, I was slowly realising, who we'd always be.

This was how the Freddie and 'Dreas show had always rolled into town, the two of us desperately clawing at each other, trying to get under each other's skin. It was the only place I belonged, with my dick buried so deep inside him that I wondered if I'd ever survive getting out of there again.

Apparently, the water heater was bigger than it used to be, as we stayed in the shower what seemed like forever, doing things we hadn't done in seven years, smelling, feeling, tasting, drinking each other in. I was glad the bathroom had been refurbished some time over the last decade, and we no longer had the flimsy shower cabinet with the broken door. Now the shower hung from the ceiling and we had solid tiles on three sides, with a wet, cold shower curtain across the opening. Well, the shower curtain was now lying in a pile next to the hamper since my legs had been attacked by the clingy fabric a third time. I didn't think I'd broken the rod, so hopefully we could reattach it and avoid any commentary when we returned to the family fold.

"You're not gay, you say?" My voice was raspy as I pushed my dick into his now well-lubed hole before pulling out and slamming into him again. And again. The moans from his throat sounded like a space opera, a mix of deep-throat voices and squeaky whimpering each time I brushed against that spot inside him. Despite my inability to make other bed partners orgasm, I knew Andreas's body better than I knew my own. I knew the things that turned him on, things that were unique to him. I knew him, and he knew me as well and pushed his arse out, repositioning his feet so I could really get that angle right.

He pressed his hands against the wall as if to hold himself up, even though I had him. I couldn't keep my hands off him—his hips, his chest, his thighs, his stomach, his shoulders, his arms, around his dick, his fingers, braiding them with mine. I couldn't get enough of him, even though I knew I wouldn't lose him ever again. Even if I let go of him now, our souls would stay together and force our bodies to follow. Soul mates. It was a weird concept that didn't exist apart from in my head, but I knew now he would always be mine.

I pressed my mouth to his neck, feeling his muscles tremble against my lips as I bit him carefully. I hadn't done it to mark him, but my body was acting on its own, making me suck on his skin, creating what I knew would be a dark, purple patch tomorrow and giving him a sweet pain he would be rewarded for later. He arched, pushing his head back, giving me access to his throat and collarbone while moving his hips faster. He controlled the speed now. I could only dig my fingers into his loins and hold tight while he rode me with jerky, desperate thrusts.

The spasms rushed through him before they started moving through me. His right hand grasped his dick while the left one curled into a fist against the wall, the knuckles white as he desperately tried to hold on to the slick surface.

We collapsed in a heap under the water, only a miracle keeping it warm. I had too many memories of getting up to have a shower when I was younger, only to discover that my fathers and sister had already used all the hot water—the drawback of being an evening person in a family of early birds.

"Maybe I am a little bit queer, then," he mumbled against my arm. We'd slumped into the corner, the water hitting our legs and spraying mist on the rest of us.

"Queer for me?" I half-joked.

"No." He shook his head and turned towards me to look me in the eye. "I'm queer, Freddie. For you and for anybody else, but it's only ever been you since we were teens. I know I said I wasn't gay back then, but I was definitely on the scale. I was so freaking stubborn, and then it confused me that I was still turned on by girls. But sex and emotions aren't the same. I was never emotionally attracted to them, not on a personal level, I mean. It's hard to explain. I didn't understand shit when being with those other men was such a failure because, you know, they should have turned me on, but I couldn't see them as sexual objects. They were too similar to you, but they weren't you, so I couldn't do them either."

"But you can do me," I teased. I knew I shouldn't. I should have supported him with kindness, said something about my feelings. Something about loving him, assured him again that it was only him for me too, even though I'd skipped around with all those other people. But I couldn't. Not now. My brain was done with serious talk when it was still struggling to process all the feelings it had encountered over the past two days. I could hardly believe it had only been two days, less than a week since I'd come home, and Andreas and I hadn't even been reunited for a full day, yet here we were, in a wet heap on the bathroom floor, my semi-limp dick sliding out of his arse.

"It's still hard to explain. The only thing that ever made sense was you. *Is* you. I suppose it doesn't matter anymore."

"It doesn't," I agreed. "We don't need to over-analyse what we feel for each other. I think...now those feelings are pretty clear."

"Okay. Ready for more?" he asked, leaning against me, squeezing his buttocks carefully around my dick.

"Perhaps not now." I smiled and kissed his neck. The love bite was red, but it would no doubt turn blue soon. "I marked you," I admitted, "because you're mine." That was as much of a declaration of love as I could muster up.

"I wanna mark you, too." He grabbed my hand and started to kiss it.

"So, matching love bites?" I giggled as his lips locked around one of my knuckles.

"Good idea." He chuckled, turning as he stretched his body against mine. He'd become taller while I'd become broader, yet we still fitted together like a pair of winter gloves. I felt his hips make a few jerky movements against me as his teeth scraped over my pec, followed by soft lips and then hard sucking that took my breath away as he absolutely gave me a bruise that I would carry for days. Proudly. He finally let go and kissed me— one of those kisses that made my head spin where we were just a fucking mess of swirling feelings and desire and belonging and all those other things I never quite understood.

"Let's get dry, shall we?" I suggested with a grin, as my stomach was rumbling. "I need breakfast." I could also smell fresh bread, which meant Frank was on his feet today, and I wanted to be there for it. With him.

"I should get Lilly to bring us breakfast in bed again," Andreas said, reluctantly moving away from me. "We used to have the two of them so well trained. Breakfast in bed in return for sweets and favours. What happened to that, eh?"

"The good old days where we could survive on sweets and shit like that for breakfast. I'm always starving these days, and luckily for us it smells like Dad has something ready to come out of the oven."

***

In the kitchen, the speakers were blasting carols—some kind of upbeat version of traditional songs. I could barely recognise the lyrics through the bass and drums, yet it still sounded festive, like a skewed version of life with a different back beat. Just like the alternative universe we found ourselves in.

The room was a mess of spillages on the floor, dirty bowls and an overflowing sink—all things that made everything look normal. Frank was working on the opposite workbench, his lean back towards us. His thin hair was even greyer, I noticed, but he was still the tall man I knew as my dad, the man I loved more than anything, the man who gave me this sting of fear of losing him every time I saw him while also filling me with immense gratitude for still being alive. I couldn't stop myself from taking the three steps forward to hug him from behind. He startled as my arms curled around him, then leant back slightly, shaking flour off his hands.

"I didn't mean to scare you," I said.

"I couldn't hear you over the music." He smiled as he turned around. "Slept well?"

"Sure. The bed is as comfy as always."

"Your toes don't freeze in there?"

"Nope."

"And you slept well too, son?" he asked Andreas.

"Yup."

"Not too cold in the basement? You know, we could probably turn up the heating a bit. I'm always warm, never feel the cold, but I know the others are always complaining about there being too little heat down there."

Andreas and I looked at each other. I thought everybody here was on top of who slept where, since the girls weren't exactly discreet when it came to hiding my secrets and our dads were all equally nosy.

Frank looked questioningly at Andreas, who parted his lips but didn't answer, probably as uncertain as me about what to say. Then Frank collapsed in laughter. "Sorry, couldn't resist. You look like you've swallowed a frog. Lovely mark you have there, Andreas."

Andreas quickly put his hand in front of his neck.

"No, further down." Frank chuckled.

Andreas rolled his eyes.

"Fredrik, there are condoms and lube sachets in the jar on your bedside table. Suppose you're old enough to bring your own, but still."

I opened my mouth in reflex to protest, my face getting hotter than the oven, but Dad just laughed again.

"Too late, son. There's a very good reason I turned up the music!"

I felt my face turn crimson. Thomas's parenting had always been slightly over the top, and Frank grasped any opportunity to take the piss out of him and his stupid supplies of condoms. Thomas didn't trust the American brands, and every time I saw him, he stuffed the familiar Norwegian brands into my bag. As it turned out, he'd stuffed the jar next to my bed full as well. Stupid grown-ups.

Andreas and I sat at the end of the long kitchen table on which stood bottles and bottles of apple juice. Frank pointed proudly to the professional-looking labels. 'Frank Juice'. I giggled and wondered if the pun reached its audience or got lost in translation, or even several puns, the way his mind worked. As well as the bottles, there plates stacked with fresh rolls with ham and cheese, Christmas bread with loads of the super-salty butter he bought at the farmer's market, and slices of brown goat's cheese—another market treat and a taste I'd missed. The industrial-dairy cheeses were milder, and those I could sometimes find in the States were so full of chemicals that they barely resembled the real thing.

I smiled at the frown on Andreas's face as I indulged in the flavours. Warm, sweet bread, melting, salty butter and the soft, slightly curdled slices of cheese made the perfect mixture in my mouth. I let out a happy sigh. "This is sooo good."

Andreas scrunched his nose and looked down at his roll. "The cheese is kind of...too sweet but not? I'm still not sure I'll ever get used to it."

"You don't like it, do you?"

"Well...I never did. Only eat it for you." He shrugged and looked at the food again.

I snagged the cheese from him and munched it. "Better now?"

He smiled at me. "Yes."

"You'll have to deal with the second-hand tastes from me then," I teased, leaning in for a kiss.

"I guess that's acceptable," he said, poking his tongue past my lips.

It didn't even feel weird, making out at the table. Not that Dad minded, laughing merrily in the corner. I wasn't fooled by his energy, though. In an hour or two, he would be drained and back in bed looking like death would claim him in a heartbeat. It scared the living daylights out of me, but it was these moments, the happy ones, that gave me peace.

Dad brought us coffee. "No more spills in the bed, kiddo." He winked. I groaned. Nothing new there. My family wasn't shy when it came to ridiculing me over everything they could, and as the rest of them slowly joined us for breakfast, the table filled with laughter and memories. We sat there for hours, the cups getting refilled as more baked goods emerged from the oven, Maria having taken over the baking duties so Frank could sit down.

Vati was moaning about not being able to get out of the doors here if we insisted on feeding him all that sugary, fat, high-carb baking. "You're baking for nine, and most of us are not bottomless stomachs anymore," he grumbled, happily picking up another biscuit and ignoring Papi's chuckle. "Sure, we're adults. But we still need to eat fifty biscuits each to get rid of this."

I looked around at the piles of treats; there must be several hundred of them.

"That'll take like...two days?" Andreas said, spluttering with crumbs as he stuffed the last piece of buttery caramel brittle between his gorgeous lips. I had to look away so my father couldn't read my mind about where those lips had been an hour ago...and where they would probably be again in another hour, or whenever we could get away from this bakery of madness. Because madness it was, a bunch of grown-ups playing at life, like we were all children and this was a sugar-coated movie.

"Frank, where did you put the cake tins?" Thomas asked, lifting another tray of steaming biscuits out of the oven.

"Cake tins..." Frank bit his lower lip and scrunched his forehead. "Ehhr..."

"In the basement perhaps?"

"No. I was tidying the basement so I moved them. If I could just remember where..." He got up and started pacing around the kitchen, opening random cupboards.

"Frank, you have hundreds of them," I said. "There's no way they're in the cupboards here. They're like...stuffed." I stood up just in time to catch a pile of plastic boxes that slid off a shelf overflowing with a mishmash of boxes and lids. "When was the last time you folks cleaned *here*?" I asked with a frown before answering my own question. "Probably never. This was Maria's lunchbox from second grade. Do you remember the unicorn devil, Dad? You painted that one, I got that T-rex football player." I smiled, looking at the old, scratched lids. "Don't throw this away. I want to keep it."

Frank frowned at the green plastic box in my hand. "I have at least sorted the boxes and lids here, I think." He looked up on the shelves again. "Maybe we can use these for the biscuits?" Then he looked between the biscuits and the boxes again. "Or not. We'd fill all of them, I guess. I'm just...I lost my train of thought."

"Why do we need biscuit tins? All these will be gone by this afternoon."
That was Maria, always the practical one.

Frank exhaled heavily and shut his eyes as if thinking. "I have no idea."

"Babe, come." Thomas was suddenly there, arms around Frank, leading him away like a confused child, which threw us all back into reality like a cold shower. Whenever I briefly forgot, it hit me even harder.

I stood there holding the damn lunchbox in my hand while Andreas started clearing the table and Vati was already loading the dishwasher. My whole world was coming to an end, and I didn't know what to do to make it stop. Christmas or not, I just wanted to cry, so I left them to it and did just that. I went to the bathroom and sat on the toilet and let my bucket of tears flow. At least I had this. My health and my sanity and my damn lunchbox. And solitude. God, I needed the silence.

Not that I got it since Andreas crept in. He knew how to manipulate the toilet door lock, a much-needed life skill in this house. He sat on the floor by my feet and didn't say a word. Just him and me. I hadn't realised how much I'd missed it, the way we functioned, how his mind worked so effortlessly alongside mine.

A short while later, the door sprang open and Maria walked in, gesturing for me to get off the loo.

"Damn it, I need to pee."

"There's a toilet in the basement. And one upstairs," Andreas pointed out, like there it would make a difference to my sister.

"Too late." She huffed and glared at me until I reluctantly got up. She didn't even wait for us to leave before she pulled down her trousers, plonked her arse on the seat and did her business. "We've grown up together, and I don't give a shit."

It would have been funny, if only it wasn't. Andreas was still sitting on the floor, and I was angrily leaning against the sink.

"You can't keep doing this," she scolded us. "We're family. We need to pull ourselves together. This is not how we deal with things."

"It's not quite a *thing*, Maria."

"It is," she countered, ripping loo paper from the roll. "It's a thing, and we need to stick together and keep our heads screwed on straight. Especially you guys." She waggled her finger at Andreas. "Fucking yourselves into oblivion is one thing, and probably a good one, for good old Fredrik here." She said it like we were discussing gym workouts. "But crying in the toilet is not going to make anything better. If anything, it makes Thomas even more antsy than he already is, and things are going to fall apart. Chin up. Get out there. Fucking try to pretend that it's Christmas, for fuck's sake."

"I wasn't crying in the toilet." Lies. Fucking lies.

She side-eyed me.

"He was," Andreas said. "And I was too. We will do better. Where do you need us?"

"Lunch." Maria pulled up her trousers and flushed the toilet. "Your Papi is attempting to peel potatoes out there, and I am not taking him to A&E when he cuts the tips off his fingers again. Get out there and take over. Bruno can be in charge of the coffee, but anything else is off limits. Thomas and Vati are taking Frank outside later, so the patio heater needs sorting out, and the living room looks like shit. Lilly and Lottie need reining in before they break something."

We did as we were told. Because you didn't argue with my sister.

We made good use of the time, cooking and laughing and keeping conversations easy, but the strange thing was, I needed... *Fuck*. I needed cuddles. Proper ones, maybe even defined as advanced cuddling when nobody was watching—if that's what one called it when you had this sudden urge to smash people into walls and tongues were involved in the same context. But in all seriousness, I needed handholding. I'd spent the last couple of years without Andreas but in desperate need of him. I realised that now, and I didn't just need him in the sexual sense. I needed someone to have my back, someone to lean on when I was falling flat on my face, which was exactly what was happening here. I was no good to anyone, but perhaps I could be. And just like that, I grabbed the back of his T-shirt, swinging him around and slammed my mouth on his. Because I could and because life required it. Andreas complained about my mouth tasting of brown cheese, but after two cups of coffee each, I guess he was just kidding.

The front door banged open, shooting another icy gust of wind into the kitchen. Apparently, Lilly still struggled to remember to close the door behind her, which was another family trait.

"Have you seen Maria and Lottie?" she demanded of nobody in particular.

"Umm..." Andreas looked at me. "They were outside earlier. Sorting candles or something?"

"No, upstairs," I said.

"Didn't they go for a walk earlier. We were going to go out, then just..."

"...postponed it!" We were finishing each other's sentences now, which was kind of cool, or maybe not.

Lilly looked between us. "Right. Well, let's hope *they* haven't forgotten about us going sledging then!" She turned to walk away, then stopped and swung back, staring at us like only she could. "Like you two obviously have." She made to leave again.

"Wait, Lilly," Andreas said, his voice soft. "How was your trip into town? I meant to come with you, but we got...distracted."

He was speaking to her in English, and she was effortlessly speaking English back. That was another thing that had changed, I realised. The way we spoke, including each other in conversations we'd previously been excluded from. I'd understood their conversations, even if they'd spoken German, but speaking it was something I couldn't do myself. I'd never known either of them in German. Andreas had never known me in Norwegian. Our life had always existed in English, and it was a habit we'd probably never break.

Smiling, she sat at the kitchen table, trailing her fingers through a pile of vegetable peelings. "It was wonderful! Really Christmassy. All the lights and the white snow...all by myself. Well, you should have come, but then. Yeah. We all know what you two were up to."

I looked at him. "Maybe we should go for a quick run into town. It's only lunchtime, so I guess the market's still in full swing."

"No, no." Lilly shook her head. "Don't go there. I mean to the market. It's just commercial shit, nothing really traditional or local." She huffed. "The snow and the lights were nice, and they were free, too. The rest is crap. So small and boring compared to the German markets," she continued, looking at Andreas. "But they did have decent gløgg."

"I'm sorry we didn't come. We'll come sledging, though. Promise." Andreas was doing all the giving here, and once again I felt like a selfish prick. I should have made an effort and not just thought of myself. I wasn't like this. I was a decent human being, but everything around me seemed overwhelming.

Lilly stood up and surveyed the mess we still needed to clear up. I'd sorted out the cupboards...well, half sorted them. The table was full of mismatched containers and lids, clip fasteners, a stray box of freezer bags, and those vegetable peels were not going to compost themselves.

"You probably won't. But hey-ho. I'll go by myself again if nobody wants to actually do Christmas properly. I mean, look at the kitchen. Let me guess.

You need me to fix this mess and lay the table. Where the hell is Vati when we need him?"

"Our parents are helping Thomas finish off a bottle of something alcoholic that looks absolutely disgusting. They're outside. So yeah, some help would be appreciated." Andreas smiled, reaching over to wipe something from my cheek. I bet it was nothing. He just wanted to touch me. I knew because all I could think of was touching him. The look of disgust from Lilly stopped me in my tracks, though.

"Come on, you two, get your heads in the game. By the way, the potatoes are boiling over."

They were too. Like everything else.

"Fredrik? Andreas? Are you there? What's happening to that lunch?" Bruno's voice came from the other side of the kitchen door.

I raised my brows at Andreas, trying to transmit, *Make them go away before they see that I can't even manage to boil potatoes*, and he shook his head, *no*, and in the middle of this wordless conversation the door banged open again.

Sometimes I wondered what it was with my family and doors. Knocking. Privacy of any sorts. Or rather Andreas's family and doors, as it was Gabriel standing on the other side, grinning cheerfully at us.

"There you are! How was the sledging?"

"Sledging?" Lilly huffed. "Nobody's been sledging. That's after lunch. We always go sledging after lunch, Vati."

"Great! I want to come. Someone has to make sure you don't break your necks!"

Bruno chuckled, appearing in a cloud of rosy cheeks and alcoholic fumes. "Seriously? Nobody is breaking anything, not limbs or hearts. I'm off duty! The only thing I will allow being broken this Christmas is glasses. You two better not have broken up already."

Andreas rolled his eyes and cast a glance at me. "Come on," he said as they all slipped into talking in German, the words running back and forth between them in that syrupy Berlin accent.

The problem was, I understood every word of that conversation, which was clearly not meant for me, and now I had no idea how to get away from it.

Chapter Nine
Bruno

He was out shovelling snow again, this time on the neighbour's drive, getting some of the frustration out of his body with the strong, firm grip he had on the shovel and the deep grunts that escaped his mouth with every shove and throw of snow. I didn't blame him. He was missing out on his daily workouts because I'd put my foot down and told him I wouldn't let him run on his own in the snow. I was being a dick, but I could just see him tripping and falling and freezing to death in the forest while I sat here worrying myself stupid. See? In my old age, Gabe's anxieties had rubbed off on me. I should have encouraged him to run. Perhaps I should have joined him outside, worked off some steam myself after that heated discussion where we kind of both lost our shit at Andreas. Perhaps I was being a bit harsh, but I knew where Gabriel stood when it came to Andreas. Andreas was just like me. He would rather run and hide than deal with the truth, and Gabriel was the badass parent. Me? I appeared chilled on the outside and now apparently worried myself sick on the inside instead of dealing with all the shit in front of me.

I suppose that was what happened when life threw you another thunderbolt and you realised that nobody was invincible, not even the incredible Frank. The Frank we'd hung out with a year ago had been his normal self, a nonstop bundle of energy and light, but the one who came to see us six months later was a wreck. So here we were, and it shouldn't have been such a shock, but fuck, life was cruel. It had made me rethink fucking everything, including battling with myself over whether I should accept the offer of working a very tempting part-time roster instead of the full-time shift pattern that was slowly killing me. I was still putting in too many hours of overtime at the hospital, but there was so much to be done, so many cases. I also wanted to go to that conference in Rome, not only because it was focused smack-bang on our field, but also because I would be able to go visit the place where my dad's ashes were scattered. Maybe. I didn't know. Gabriel would come with me. He had some overtime he could cash in, and...

I wasn't losing it. I was just so tired, and this trip was everything I'd hoped it would be. It always was. Spending some quality time with Thomas was a mood lifter in itself. He'd just sit there and let me talk rubbish about advanced stitch technology and skin-graft improvements using lab-grown skin mesh. Then he'd tell me about astrophysics topics he no longer understood and research I barely comprehended, and we'd both laugh at each other's shortfalls. He made good coffee. We made the silences comfortable. We balanced each other out in a seemingly impossible friendship that had lasted longer than I'd ever thought possible when I booked that holiday all those years ago. I'd gained a brother. Gabriel had gained a family. I'd picked up two stray kids who made me just as proud as my own. Maria called me Papi and sent me messages almost every day. She had a group chat called *#Daddyissues* where she treated us four dads to daily snippets from her teaching career, memes and screenshots of her students' exam answers that always made me chuckle.

It was a different kind of tiredness here, where everything was magically beautified by the snow, the darkness, the twinkling lights everywhere and the candles in every window. It calmed my soul, took the pressure off. I looked around at the framed photos on the walls, many of them telling the story of the last ten years of this family—a family we were now fully part of. There was no doubt about that. We were all in those photos, and they were in the photos all over our fridge door at home too. We were entwined on social media, and our kids loved each other. Well, some more than others judging by the sounds coming from the other side of the kitchen.

"Frank, turn the music up, mate?" I shouted as Thomas sighed deeply, momentarily looking up from his tablet.

"Yo, Bruno!" Frank stomped into the living room carrying a tray and a bowl that no doubt contained something diabetes inducing. "Make those hands useful and roll this out into forty small balls."

"How do you like your balls?" I asked with a cheeky wink.

"In pairs. You of all people should know this." He winked back. "Firm and a little hairy."

"Ugh. I think I'll stick to your dough balls here. What flavour?" I nipped at a piece of dough and let the sweet, buttery gunk fill my mouth.

"Salted caramel. Maria just found a new recipe."

"Frank…" Thomas groaned. "You're going to kill us with all these biscuits."

"Chill, baby." Frank smiled and flicked some dough off his hands towards Thomas. "These are for the nurses to take back to base, and anyway, it keeps me sane. Just something to do. I have two more rounds for you to deliver to the food bank later. Should I do some for the Shelter project?"

"You should come and sit down and watch a movie."

"You and my man Bruno here are just waiting for that, eh? The moment I sit down to watch something and then you'll force me to watch *Die Hard*, and my blood pressure will go through the roof."

"It is not de proper Christmas until Hans Gruber has fallen off de Nakatomi Plaza, you know that, Frank," I said in my best German accent.

"Ho-ho, Motherfucker!" he replied and disappeared back out into the kitchen, leaving me with dough all over my hands and a smile on my face.

"It's *Yippekayee, Motherfucker*," Thomas muttered, grabbing a handful of dough out of the bowl, smiling at me as he shook his head. "Pass me that plate," he said and shuffled closer to me on the sofa so he could reach, grabbing more dough from my hand and placing it in a lump directly on the coffee table.

"Food hygiene," I whispered.

"Fuck off, Dr Moretti. No scrubs allowed. It's Christmas."

"We don't want to give those poor nurses dodgy biscuits," I argued, smiling broadly as he gave me a pretend-shocked look.

"My home is sparkling clean. I can assure you of that," he hissed, drawing his face into a supposedly offended expression that made me laugh out loud.

"Just roll your balls and shut up," I snickered, kneading the dough between my fingers.

"Roll your own balls and shut up," he retaliated, and we settled into a quiet, easy rhythm.

"Thomas, how's Fredrik doing?" I asked after a while. I had to because the state of my own son worried me no end right now. The girls were doing great. They were open and honest and flew by the moment. Nothing fazed them, and I thanked whoever was in charge of the world that neither of them seemed to have inherited my damn depressive genes or Gabriel's constant doubts and worries. Andreas, though—he'd got it all.

"He's coping, I think. I know we've talked about this before, but Andreas is, all things considering, good for him. Fredrik's a lot like Frank in that way. He doesn't always understand it, but he needs someone to take care of him, to push him when necessary and calm him when he goes into overdrive. Fredrik's been unhappy, probably more so in the last year. He's lost his sparkle, the drive in his research. He says it's felt like he's on autopilot, and that's never good. Not in his field."

"I know that feeling. I get it at work sometimes, when it all seems to lack sense, and I question why the hell I've just spent nine hours in surgery when it won't make a damn bit of difference in the end."

"You save lives," he said, staring at me like only Thomas could, when he wanted you to listen. Really listen.

"Not always. Sometimes things go horribly wrong. Sometimes we make things worse."

"It's very similar in research. You can spend months on a project for it all to fall flat. It makes you feel like a fool for even thinking you were on to something. But you save lives. You try to make things better. Like that woman from last week you told me about, who bled out on the table after giving birth and everyone said to call it, apart from you. You had hope. You pushed. She lived to see another day. She might still be very unwell, but that family are celebrating Christmas this week, and you did that. It was your call."

"I didn't want to call it," I said, feeling my chest go tight. "All I could think was, my Gabriel once lay on that table. He made it. I couldn't let someone else's life shatter. Not on my shift."

"I know," Thomas said quietly, and for a while the silence resumed, just us and the mounting pile of dough balls.

"Andreas is suffering," I admitted. "He's twenty-seven and lives at home. He can't settle down, never even tries to find someone. I can see it in him. He lives in the past, churning over a stupid mistake he made when he was at his lowest, over and over again like he can't forgive himself. He loves your boy. We all do. I just don't want Fredrik to feel pressured into starting up something that will break them both if it goes wrong."

"I told Frank it was a mistake to make Andreas come. Perhaps we should have let Fredrik settle back into life here before forcing the boys to spend time together."

"Wouldn't have made a blind bit of difference, Thomas. They would have done this, however life panned out. And..." I couldn't say it—the thing we didn't really talk about.

"He needed to be here. We all know that." Thomas's voice was barely above a whisper.

It never failed to amaze me how much strength sat in Thomas's bones, how well he held everything together. I kept asking him if he needed a breather, if there was anything I could do to ease the burden he was carrying, but he always shook his head, almost in desperation.

"I need to do what I need to do," he'd say. "Another day, in the future, that's when I will allow myself to crumble. That's when I'll need you, mate. For now, though, just let me do this. Just having you guys here keeps me sane."

"I know, and I've got you."

I knew how that felt, the insane fear that lived in your bones, the weight that threatened to crush your chest with every wheezing breath. It was safer to talk about the boys, the weather, roll dough into balls.

"Andreas needed to see that it wasn't as bad as he was making it out in his head. That the two of them have always been like this. They function well when they are together. When they are not..."

"Their lives fall apart," Thomas finished dryly. We could both have expanded on that conversation, but there was a time and a place for those words, and it wasn't here.

"They're both adults," I said. "If they didn't want to be here, they wouldn't be."

"Yeah, I know."

"And it's good for Gabriel to be here too."

"It always is."

"Are you able to reply with a sentence containing more than three words?"

"Fuck off and roll your damn balls, man."

"Fuck you." I laughed.

We went back to our comfortable silences. It was enough just to know he was there.

Chapter Ten
Andreas

I'D FELT ALMOST high all day, high on endorphins and sex and him. He'd always had that effect on me, even when we were barely out of our teens. He looked at me and I would shiver. He idolised me, I kind of knew that, but it had subtly changed to something else, and that was a whole new world of feelings to frighten the living daylights out of me.

In a way, I'd always seen it in my parents. Co-dependency. I used to pride myself on not needing anyone. I was independent. Making my own way in the world. Yeah, right. Look where that got me. I'd had that big epic breakdown, and as soon as I'd surfaced and started riding the waves of life again, I'd slipped, hit rock bottom with a heavy thud. Again and again. You learned to live with it after a while, climbing up to the surface, your hands bloodied from the rockface, and then slipping under again, slicing open every healing wound. It sounded dramatic when I tried to explain it, but I suppose that was me. Anxiety. Good days. Bad days. Fucking awful days.

Papi had lived with it all his life, and he'd still managed to become everything I admired. He was respected. People travelled from all over to have a consultation with Dr Moretti, the world-renowned expert in gender reassignment and specialist gynaecological care. Post-partum repairs, vaginoplasty, all those complex procedures that instilled respect and awe, but then you'd meet Papi and his right-hand man Doctor Martino and wonder how the hell anyone let the two of them near a scalpel. They spoke loud, animated Italian at each other and drank red wine, and all hell would break loose.

Vati loved Dr Martino. And his hubby. The dude had apparently been some kind of elite model in his heyday. I kept thinking I should google him sometime and find out what else he did in his youth because I couldn't really see it. He was handsome, fine, but nothing special. Not like...not like the blond Viking scooting over so I could crawl back into bed with him, fully clothed, like we hadn't just spent ten minutes making the bed just so we could dirty it up again.

"Talk to me," Freddie said, and his whole body felt tense. Not good.

"What have I done now?" I asked weakly, feeling about ten years old.

"Honesty. Your Vati just hated on me big time."

"Vati adores you. What kind of bullshit is that?"

"He said I can't handle you and that you'll ruin my life. That you can't look after yourself, let alone start a long-distance relationship with someone who doesn't trust a word coming out of your mouth."

I sighed, but he was right. And it was true: my parents had told me off too, warned me that I was once again rushing headfirst in something that had a fifty-fifty chance of ending in a disaster I couldn't afford. The odds were stacked against me, and we all knew it. Even Freddie.

"Vati is overreacting..." I started, but then I turned over so I was face-to-face with him. I tangled my fingers in his hair, and he mirrored my movements, his hand coming to a rest at the back of my neck. "Vati's also right. I'm twenty-seven years old, and I don't do well living on my own. I tried, Freddie. I moved away for Uni, and I fucked up. Took me two years longer than everyone else to finish my degree because I was lonely and stupid most of the time. I missed my family. I struggled financially and didn't have the guts to ask for help. I was never like you, all organised and sensible. Papi and Vati kept asking if I was okay, and I wasn't, but I couldn't tell them."

"We all make mistakes and struggle," Freddie said. "Don't think that my time in America has been a bed of bloody roses." As he spoke, he stroked my skin, and it soothed me. Like, he might have been pissed off with me, but we were still okay. So far.

"I got myself a job and a flat," I said. "Spent almost a year living there, and things were getting better. I was good at my job, I liked my colleagues, and I signed up for some more courses to complete my degree. I saw my supervisors and the behavioural therapists working, and I wanted that. I wanted to do what they did. For the first time in my life, I had direction, and it felt good, you know? Took on a load of extra shifts, studied like crazy and then failed the first exam. I don't have to tell you what happened next."

"I might have been silent in your life, Andreas, but I always knew what was going on. I know you got evicted when you defaulted on your rent despite having cash in the bank. Lilly was crying on the phone because you just wouldn't listen. She told me she was moving in with you to look after you, and then she rang me all distraught because of the state of you."

"I think I'm missing that adult gene. The one where you kind of go all sensible and figure all your shit out."

"You're fine, baby," he said in that soothing voice of his and held me tighter than he needed to. "That was one of those moments when I half packed my bags to fly home and go sort you out. Then I remembered you didn't love me anymore and I wouldn't be welcome."

"I *always* loved you, even when I was too messed up to remember that I did. And you always told me how much you struggled with your dad, how he scared you, and how you always worried he would one day fall off the edge of sanity. I didn't want you to have to worry about me too. I told Vati and Papi not to say anything to you. I begged them."

"Yeah, well, you know what our parents are like. They're the biggest gossip queens in the world. Everything moves around this family like wildfire. I eventually find out everything, apart from something about a threesome? I was never told about that." He leant in and kissed my lips. "And that's okay."

"It's not. I will mess up again. I will do something stupid and forget to pay my phone bill or something. I failed my driving test because I forgot to turn up. I can't be trusted to do anything."

"You can. Just don't sign up for any more threesomes. No more hook-ups. No more."

"I made up some funny stories about that threesome, to make everyone laugh. The truth..." I snorted. I hated this. I hated that I was so weak and stupid.

"Tell me," he said softly.

"I... We didn't even get our clothes off. She kissed me and I burst into tears. End of. I sat on their sofa and sobbed my eyes out. Then I went home and googled how to die from embarrassment because I was pretty sure that was the end of me. I deleted my Grindr and Tinder and everything. That was a pretty low moment, even for me."

It was nice to see him smile. See the dimples in his cheeks form. Feel the little kisses he placed all over my forehead.

"Yet you go to work and run a whole department of mental health nurses, and you're in charge of...is it three group homes?"

"I'm not in charge of shit. Well, I make sure we have the right people in the right places at the right time. Funny that. And yeah. I manage that. I get up in the morning and go to work. I think because I love it. I enjoy what I do. It helps. And I still haven't fucked that part up."

"Your Vati said you were about to epically fuck all of this up."

"I'm not. I wouldn't let anything happen to you. Not ever. Not now. But..."

"Yes?"

"I can't do long distance. I can't do this with you here and me in Berlin."

"We're not doing long distance," he said matter-of-factly. "I'm too old for that shit. I want you with me. We need to find somewhere to live, and I need to get a job."

"I...I can't just resign," I said, and my voice was full of dread. This wasn't easy. Honesty was fucking hard, and being an adult was not everything it was made out to be.

"Tell me what you need, Andreas."

"A blow job."

"Now?"

"Nah, just trying to buy myself a minute of courage."

That made him sigh and roll his eyes. Just like his father. It was funny how alike they were. Uncle Thomas kept this whole family stable, micromanaging us all even though he would never own up to it, dropping carefully plotted schedules into our inboxes, usually the first week of January, detailing holiday weeks, birthdays, Christmas, lists.

"If I just upped and left, my kids, the patients I work with, their families— it would set them back weeks. Months even. I couldn't do that. I love those people. They rely on me to be there, to work with them, and keep their schedules. These things are rigid. It's how they tick."

"I know that. That's fair," he said slowly, tasting the words while I knew his brain was ticking over, trying to find a solution.

"I've got savings, Freddie. I'm not completely useless, throwing us out there with no plan. If you...I mean, if you would consider it, I could rent somewhere and keep us both happy. You could study German or something. Find a job. Just for a few months so I could introduce the person who would take over and set everything up. Make sure everything runs smoothly. After that, I would go with you, anywhere you wanted to go. If you want to go back to America—"

"I don't care," he said sternly. "I will go anywhere you are. If you need to be in Berlin, I will come to you."

That hadn't even been on my list of options. Freddie didn't belong in Berlin. Well, apart from in my bed.

"We barely know each other anymore. What if after a few weeks you get pissed off with me?"

We both laughed. It was a comforting sound, though, with his body pressed tightly against mine and his hands around my face.

"You need to be *here*, Freddie. With your family. You need to be with Frank. That's why you came home in the first place."

"I came home because there was nothing left of me in the States. There was nothing there, and I was drained. I wanted to come home to be with Dad, yeah, but that was just the trigger that shot the bullet. I've been back, what. A week? It's made me angry."

"Angry?" I shifted in our embrace, gave myself a bit of safe distance. He closed it again, kissing my forehead. He did that and I melted. Every time.

"I should have done it years ago. Cut the stubborn bullshit and stopped running away. I came home because I had nowhere left to run anymore. And somehow, the thought of you coming here, it was so bloody overwhelmingly terrifying that it had almost become inevitable. Like the big bang. Why, 'Dreas? Why did we wait so long? Why did we waste all these years when we could just...I don't know? Why?"

"We did it because we both needed to grow up. Figure out who we were when we weren't the flipping 'Dreas and Freddie soap opera of constant drama. So we tried to grow up and we became exactly the same people we were before. Stupid, I know."

He laughed. I loved his laughter, I always had. I loved his bad stubble that needed to come off, the messy frizzy hair on his head, those eyes that always stabbed me with honesty. I loved all of him, and I'd never questioned his love for me because he wore it like a freaking coat.

"I'm moving to Berlin, and then we'll figure it out. Wherever we can both work and live and be happy. That's where we'll settle." He said like it was a done deal. "Like throwing darts at a map. Find a random place and just go for it?"

"Somewhere close to both our families. Copenhagen?"

"I have to learn Danish?"

"You need to learn German first," I murmured and painted a line on his nose with my tongue.

"I took advanced German for three years, you arsehole," he replied in perfect German, stunning me into silence. "So shut your gob and kiss me."

Chapter Eleven
Fredrik

I WOKE UP early on 'the day before the day', as we called it here, and I already knew, minute by minute, how the day would pan out.

First, there would be too many of us trying to be the manager of the getting-the-tree-inside job. Thomas and Bruno had picked it up yesterday, and the poor tree was now on the terrace, right outside the living room. It would soon be moved downstairs into the cool basement for a few hours before we dragged it back upstairs again and into the living room. The entire process was always messy, with a lot of wet spots of melted snow on the floor and sticky sap on our fingers. We always argued about whether we actually needed to carry it downstairs, since it was never really that cold outside anyway, so perhaps we could just move it one metre inside and water it with ice-cold water and that'd be it. Stupid, but it was tradition. It was what we did.

Next, we'd get the boxes of ornaments and decorations and open them and talk about them, and my dads would get teary-eyed when they found certain ones that carried memories, like the old hearts with rainbow flags and all the ornaments they had given each other every year since forever. Then they would cry out loud when Maria and I opened our boxes with the ornaments we'd been gifted ever since we were babies, and they would say, like they had said for the last ten years, that we should take them home with us after Christmas so we could decorate our own trees with them. We all knew that would never happen. Well, now I was hoping I'd one day need them for another tree somewhere—in Berlin or Göttingen or Copenhagen or wherever we'd end up. I'd already emailed around my network of students and professors late last night, asking if they knew of any open positions in Germany. I wasn't even sure I wanted to continue down the research route, but it was worth a try, and some of those people had connections outside academia too.

I was surprising myself even thinking that because that part had definitely not been in my plan a week ago. A week ago, I was wallowing in self-pity and desperation, trying to find anything to hold on to and I hadn't thought I'd need a plan, yet here I was. Making one, like a fool. Then I'd walked into my dad's bedroom and thrown it all out the window because fucking hell, I wasn't going anywhere.

Anyway, back to today. After the tree was decorated, we would dash around the house looking for our gifts, and at least one of us would panic because they couldn't find something that was probably sat here in plain sight, and then we would pile gifts under the tree for tomorrow evening, whining and complaining that there were too many and it was too much and that we shouldn't consume so much and were too old for gifts and yet we'd all get a load each. Mine were in a huge box downstairs: I'd ordered them and had them delivered here. I'd even ordered something for Andreas, in a panic. I blushed, trying to remember what on earth I'd bought him. Stupid socks probably. Something that meant nothing.

Someone would always hurry out to get some gifts they had forgotten. I guess that would be me this year. Getting something proper for Andreas. It had been Maria and Lottie last year, the two of them panic-buying weird shit in a disorganised frenzy. I already knew Lilly had her gifts here—she'd told me about some of them yesterday—and Thomas had their stuff in order. Frank had never forgotten to get Thomas's gift, not even in his worst periods, so that was all probably fine too.

And then we'd have rice porridge for dinner, and someone would find the almond and get a marzipan pig. When Maria and I were kids, we probably got more than our share and even one each of the almond gifts, but our dads were always really bad losers and wouldn't let us win the race for the almond without a good fight. It was the same with board games. Someone always had to win—the one with most luck or the superior skills but never the youngest or the one who had the most to lose. Thomas and Frank had been really strict on that, no cheating to let us win. So yeah. There would be drama over some stupid board game, one Maria had researched the shit out of that had won awards or some crap like that. We had piles of them in the basement—games none of us ever fully grasped or understood—but we'd still play them or at least try to.

In the evening, we would try to gather in front of the TV to watch *Kvelden før Kvelden*—the traditional pre-Christmas show that the Norwegian state television would never dare to remove from the TV listings on *the evening before the evening*. It was a must-watch: if they didn't broadcast it, there would be an uproar from the Norwegian population.

That would be us, all huddled together on the couch. It had worked better when we were younger and Andreas and I had inevitably been cuddled up at one end of the huge corner sofa, with Lilly and Lottie curled against our legs and Maria next to them, Gabriel and Bruno at the other end and Frank and Thomas in the chairs or running back and forth with more snacks and drinks. Over time, we'd drifted together to a union, with all of us getting up and about to do things. And we'd grown. The couch was no longer big enough for all of us. It would probably end up in a pillow fight, and Gabriel would join in at first even if he was always the one questioning the safety of everything, and then Bruno would start hitting him, so softly, and Frank would yell at us and call us fuckwits before joining in too, and Thomas would just smile at how silly we all were.

The show itself—it was obviously dull, mainly in a language only four of us spoke, which was probably why none of us really knew what it was about, but the fact that we sat there, together, always got us in the mood.

And if the show was too bad, one could always get up to help Frank set the table or get more biscuits or wine for everyone. But when *Dinner for One* started, everyone was suddenly in front of the TV with their sherry glasses. However stupid it was, it was tradition, and we loved it. I always had, even as a child.

But before all this, I needed to get rid of the warm, soft squid entangled with my body. I had an arm across my chest and his legs were entwined with mine. I wasn't surprised to find that I wasn't wearing my boxers nor that his hot crotch was squished against mine. His other arm supported my neck, and when I tried to move, my hair got stuck between his fingers.

I kissed him, smiling when he giggled at my lips tickling his shoulder. I couldn't move with my arms around him, one dead under his ribcage, the other resting across his hips with my fingers spread at the top of his buttocks, but if I wiggled a bit, I was pretty sure he'd wake up with a finger in his arse.

So, I wiggled a bit.

And then the day passed exactly like I knew it would.

Kidding.

He was still asleep, so I just lay there and looked at him. Watched his chest slowly rise and fall, little bubbles forming between his lips with each breath. He was...Andreas, the boy I'd met at sixteen, who had forever since monopolised every cell in my body. But he also wasn't that Andreas anymore, and I hated myself for thinking it. He wasn't traditionally handsome, too thin in some places, too thick in others. His ears stuck out, and he always looked like he needed a haircut. These days, in his adult self, he still struggled to grow a beard, so his chin was patchy with stubble, and his eyebrows...well, let's just say Maria had more than once threatened him with her tweezers.

But he was mine, and he made me irrationally happy.

Which, again, made me do a complete U-turn in my head because who the hell was I kidding?

I'd handed in all my resignations, sold my meagre belongings and sat my sorry arse on a plane home, fully expecting my head to be a dangerous place for the next year. I'd never had to deal with loss. Grief. Not like this. I'd worried about my dad most of my life, but this was a completely different ball game, and my whole body seemed to spasm in painful jerks just thinking those thoughts. The only thing that kept me sane, right here, right now, was the future, knowing that whatever happened, I'd have Andreas. But would I trade him for the chance of having more time with my dad?

I had to get up before the panic in my chest got to me and I just wanted to scream. Which I did, but in the more controlled setting of the local running tracks. I'd borrowed Thomas's gear, and his running shoes were far too tight for my feet, but I needed to get out. Get air in my lungs. Clear my head.

As it turned out, my head was already surprisingly clear, but I still screamed into the snow-covered pine trees as wet snowflakes landed on my face. They could easily have been tears because the emotions in my chest were making it difficult to breathe.

The future was simple. I needed to grab hold of that man in my bed and make him promise. Perhaps I should propose, drag him down to the register office and stick a virtual ring on his finger. Well. Andreas didn't own a suit.

He had always been the dude in threadbare clothes, the guy in the dirty T-shirt, fringe covering his eyes and a cheeky smile on his face.

Told you, my future was straightforward. I couldn't even think straight.

I was smiling as I kicked the ice from the soles of my shoes and stepped back into the heat. A home, my home, where Maria and Vati were already sorting out the food, and candles were lit in the windows.

I grabbed a shower and, for the first time in days, had a nice, comfortable shave. It was like looking at a different person in the mirror, someone who had his head together. Funny the difference a week could make.

Frank was up, pottering around with a cup and his dressing gown tightly wrapped around his thin frame. I kind of half hugged, half tried to swing him around the room before I was told to sit down and sort out the cabbage. It was something to do with my hands when everything around me seemed intent on drowning my temporary truce with myself and my feelings. I was allowed to be happy. For once, I was. Things may not be like this tomorrow, but I wanted this now. I wanted this bubble of having my family around me, where Thomas was smiling and Frank was laughing and Maria was telling them off and at the same time putting a cup of coffee in my hands. Where Lilly kissed my cheek and Vati was laughing, and there was Andreas walking around like a zombie with his hair in a complete mess.

He was wearing my hoodie.

And it made me happy.

Then the Christmas tree got its trip to the basement and ended up leaning slightly towards the window with too many of us trying to make it look straight. None of us had ever been straight. We were messy and bent and crooked, all with our flaws, but even that made me happy.

Frank and Thomas had their moment over the ornament box, trembling fingers clutching at the old hearts and bulbs and figures, tender kisses, glittering eyes, laughter and more kisses. Frank got a hilariously ugly Marvel figure from Thomas, and Thomas got a small, green, glittering Christmas tree that looked suspiciously like a butt plug decorated with sequins and pearls and with obvious threads of glue gun remains. I didn't hear everything he said to Frank, as he blushed and lowered his voice, but I heard him say something like, "No, Frank, it's not..." and I was absolutely sure I didn't want to hear the rest of it. Because...ewww.

Andreas helped me put the ornaments from my box on the tree, and we looked at each other and I think we both thought the same when Frank muttered that we'd needed to buy more ornaments because the tree looked positively bare, which was patently false, but it made us laugh.

Maria seemed to have forgotten to bring some gifts, so after a while she started sneaking down to the dads' wine cellar with a pile of gift bags to steal wine, but Thomas caught her in the act and calmly told her that her gifts were under her bed in her room and wasn't she supposed to have vacuumed before Lilly and Lottie arrived, so why hadn't she found them already?

The pile under the tree was huge. It was hardly under the tree, more like molten lava running all along the huge veranda windows, effectively barring a visit from Santa Claus from that direction. Luckily, we were all too old for that now. Maybe we'd be the ones to surprise the neighbouring kids one day. Maybe we'd have our own. It was funny the things that were suddenly running through my head.

Frank found the almond in the porridge, and as always, he shared the huge marzipan pig Bruno and Gabriel had brought between us. The soft Lübecker Marzipan was so much better than the dry, sweet marzipan we usually got here in Norway—another thing that made things real. The taste on my tongue brought me back to memories that somehow made my chest ache less.

Once dinner was eaten and cleared away, we started setting the dinner table for the next day, which was insane, but it was the way we did it. My grandparents' best china, nice and stylish, with a white linen tablecloth and golden place mats, regular white plates for the main meal because that one year we used Grandma's old porcelain, the plates remained unwashed for a week and started to smell because nobody wanted to be the one to break the antique dishes. Everyone had been in a party mood, and things obviously didn't get better over the week, but in the end, Bruno did it. My dads gave him a bottle of wine from the year he was born afterwards.

The silverware was probably even older and was not allowed into the dishwasher, but we all threw it in there anyway, along with the good cups and the glasses that were a mishmash of crystal we'd gathered over the years. "It all goes into the dishwasher at least once," Frank had said with a shrug. Not all of it twice, though. Nothing matched anymore since we tended to break at least one glass each in December, and now everyone was arguing and there was too-loud music and the girls were squealing, and I just couldn't cope.

As always, I was left to fold the napkins, and as always, I only knew how to turn them into some kind of uneven, badly shaped fan.

"Come on, surely you can fold them into swans?" Andreas laughed and looked at the crumpled napkin in my hands. "All those degrees and you didn't take advanced table setting at one of those fancy universities you went to?"

"Sure. Got a master's degree in napkin folding," I answered with a straight face.

He kissed me, and I smirked, but my body was once again tense. I wasn't used to this many people having their noses in my business. Too close. Too many cuddles, too many hands on my body and too much sensory overload. I felt strangled, suffocated by the emotions inside of me as well as the pressure to give everyone around me what they needed, or what I *thought* they needed. Suddenly I felt like everyone wanted a piece of me, and right now I couldn't even keep hold of myself.

Lilly and Lottie were standing next to the table, staring expectantly at us. I ignored them, trying to force my napkin into some kind of recognisable shape or at least something resembling the video Andreas had just loaded up on YouTube.

"So...napkin folding," one of them said. I could hear the chuckle in her voice.

"Yes. That's pretty gay, isn't it, 'Dreas?"

"Yes. But I guess they are gay then."

I glared at them as if looks could kill. I could only hope. They'd also polished off a whole bottle of some sickly-sweet liquor earlier.

"Oh, he's cute," Lottie continued, looking at her sister.

"Who's cute?" Maria peeked in from behind.

"Your gay brother."

"Is he? Never thought of him like that."

"He's obviously gay."

"No, cute, I mean."

"He's gay *and* cute. Gays are cute."

"That's kind of a generalisation, isn't it?" Maria was taking the piss.

"Yes, but he *is* cute. They both are. They're a cute couple." I couldn't even tell who was speaking.

I scrunched up the cursed napkin and threw it on the table. "Enough!" I spat at them with venom in my voice. "Do the damned napkins yourself, princesses."

I turned to Andreas, who was trying and failing to disguise a giggle "What are you laughing at?" I hissed.

"Nothing. Come on, let's go," he said, grabbing my arm as he got up.

I followed him without hesitation. Another day I might have questioned why, but today I'd had enough of my family. There had been too many people, too much nosiness, too many unasked questions, too much walking around me as if they'd known about us for years, which was annoying since we'd been a 'we' for less than twenty-four hours.

Another fucking lie.

Andreas had me by both arms, pushing me through the overcrowded living room to the hallway, putting my coat on me and feeding my feet into my boots before knotting a long, striped scarf around my neck. He dressed himself, too, his dark-green cap, a grey scarf that looked as soft as his skin...

"You should go sit down. You didn't even finish your wine."

"Plenty of time to finish it later." He spoke into his lap, trying to tie his shoelaces.

"It's Christmas." I didn't know what else to say, how to make things calm in my head again.

"Yes, and you've had enough and need a break. So we're going for a walk."

"What about the rest of them? Everyone will be wondering where we've gone."

"You're more important, and you need to destress before you have a coronary. We can't have that because according to our sisters, I apparently can't live without you." He leaned in to kiss me. His lips tasted of wine and caramel biscuits and chocolate. He tasted like *him*, and it made me want to cry. "Come on." He nodded to the door.

I knew where he was taking me the second we turned left outside the house. We were walking fast, in a coordinated rhythm without marching in step, each leading the other, our hands attached. I braided his fingers with mine, wanting to feel as much of him as I could, glad we didn't put on gloves even though the evening was cold. *Really not a night to sleep in the basement*, I thought with a tingle in my belly, glad I'd be saving him from that. Or maybe he was saving me.

The evening was dark, the golden glow hovering beneath the streetlamps making the road seem calm and quiet. We had walked for a few minutes and had yet to see even a stray cat, let alone any people.

"We should have brought a torch," I muttered as we turned onto the small, gravelled path.

"Nah, we'll find the way." Andreas squeezed my hand in reassurance. He looked up at the half moon and then at me. "You're my light anyway." He laughed. "It's true. I'm not just quoting bad poetry at you, Mr Strand."

"That's cheesy, Herr Fischer-Moretti."

"Herr Moretti-Fischer—so pompous. I might take your name one day. Andreas Strand. Easy. Even in German." He smiled at me.

"Works in any language." I smiled back and rested my head on his shoulder. He kissed my cheek, probably rolling his eyes at my lifelong tease. His name was ridiculous. As ridiculous as mine was. Full of stories and connected lives, names entwined that would tell the history of a love that had lasted a lifetime. "At least we have the moon." He nodded towards the now bright path between the trees. It wasn't far; we weren't going into the middle of the forest, just about fifty metres in. This had always been my secret forest when I was a kid, where I'd run around with my friends and played whatever we'd played then, except football because that had been played in the field on the other side of the main road.

The first time I brought Andreas here was to escape my nosy dads and sister, when he'd visited me alone the year after we met. It was the only place I could imagine bringing him right then, far enough away to hide, close enough to not explode from the heat filling my tight jeans. I'd ejaculated minutes later behind the large stone, resting my back against it with his head between my thighs. I'd made him sit on the stone afterwards, so I could reciprocate. We'd been too terrified of being caught at home and even more terrified of being found here by anyone walking past.

From then on, this kind of became our place, even though we never had sex here again. After all, it was pretty close to the neighbours, but it was a nice place to hide away for a while, to just sit there without saying anything, being together.

The stone was covered in snow, so we stood next to it, our hands entwined. The first kiss tasted of cold, cold air, cold lips, cold nose, his jacket cold under my hands, and I couldn't slide them under his clothes to feel him, so I clung to his clothes instead.

He bent his head back and exposed his neck. I eagerly nipped at it, planting small kisses over his warm skin, sniffing him, licking a cold stripe along the carotid artery while he pulled me closer. "Look," he whispered and nudged me.

The sky above us was suddenly covered in rolling waves of colour. The green was almost fluorescent, drifting towards the other colours in the spectrum, yellow, orange, red, almost pink, then blue and violet on the other side.

I'd never seen aurora this bright and colourful before. When we'd visited Svalbard with my dad once during winter, we'd seen it, but only in stark green. Above Oslo, I'd hardly ever noticed it. There was usually too much light pollution, but tonight it somehow felt darker, or perhaps it was because we were far enough from the light not to be blinded by it. Sometimes you had to see the darkness to actually appreciate the light.

A bit like life. I'd had to lose him to understand my loss. Again, my thoughts made me well up, and I clawed at his jacket. It was easier to just not think and try to clear my head, let the spectacle above me take centre stage.

I'd always loved the complex mystery behind auroras. On one hand, they were easy, the result of disturbances in the magnetosphere caused by solar wind. These disturbances were sometimes strong enough to alter the trajectories of charged particles in both solar wind and magnetospheric plasma. These particles, mainly electrons and protons, precipitate into the upper atmosphere, and the resulting ionisation and excitation of atmospheric constituents emit light of varying colour and complexity.

Easy.

The colours were also easy. Light had different wavelengths at different altitudes, so sometimes it would become red and sometimes blue and sometimes the wavelengths were in between and the colours became different.

But still, my colleagues lacked the full understanding of the physical processes which led to different types of auroras. We could observe it and see what happened, but not know precisely why and how, and despite my desire to understand nature, I'd always found this lack of explanation weirdly fascinating. Perhaps like real life, nature didn't always give us all the answers.

"This is completely unique," I murmured, still in awe. His cheek was warm against mine, despite the bitter cold. "It's not like the star constellations."

He looked at me, full of questions.

"We can stand in different places on Earth and basically see the same stars. The ceiling might be different, but whenever we both see a star or a constellation from where we are, we will see it in the same way. But auroras are different. They will never be the same again, and if we move they will be different. So even if we both look at auroras at the same time, they will be different auroras."

"I don't understand anything you're saying, but I love when you talk science to me. I love...that you love it."

"It's truly unique. This moment will never be here again. Everything is constantly changing."

That thought stabbed me in the guts again, reminding me that in this moment we were truly all alone in the world. I pulled him closer and just held him, standing still, looking at the colourful bands dancing over our ceiling, the white clouds of our breaths in the darkness, and slowly the feeling of being alone disappeared. Because I wasn't, and I'd decided I didn't want to be.

Nothing would ever be the same again. Life was constantly changing. All we had was life right now. The breaths that we were taking in this forest, his hand in mine. It was too much to grasp. Too heavy for my fragile head.

When we got back home again, things felt considerably calmer inside. The TV was off; carols played low in the background. Lilly and Lottie quietly folded napkins at the table, giggling in front of a laptop showing some intricate folding procedure. Andreas went downstairs, saying he had to get something out of his bag, and I found myself in the kitchen with my sister.

Maria was emptying the dishwasher, which had run for the umpteenth time today. Baking bowls were stacked on the bench; as usual, Dad hadn't had the energy to clean them.

"Where is everyone?" I asked, taking the pile of plates she handed me and putting them on the upper shelf in the cupboard.

"The dads went out for a drive—Frank wanted air—and Gabriel and Bruno have gone to bed." She lifted her eyebrows.

"And the Ls are folding napkins?" I asked with a frown.

"Yeah. They didn't want to wait for you." She smiled. "Look, I'm sorry if we offended you. It really wasn't our intention. We were just...being silly."

I smiled back and shook my head. "No, no problem. I'd just had enough. Too many people."

"Yes." She looked at the bowls behind her and the army of mugs next to the sink. "Nine people are quite a lot...of people."

"Takes a teacher to manage a group our size," I joked. "It's only half a class, though."

"Ha-ha, very funny."

I looked at her, probably for the first time this Christmas, properly. She was beautiful, my sister. Green eyes, like me, curly hair, dimples, her skin for once bare, free from all that make-up and glitter. Just her, the way she was.

"How are you, Maria?" I asked.

"Fine," she answered, a bit too quickly. "Why?"

"I'm just worried. I care about my big sister."

Her smile deepened the dimples. "So you do? Care?"

"Yes, I do. I'm not always good at showing it, but I do."

"It's a lot to deal with. I don't want to talk about it."

"Neither do I, but at some point, we'll have to."

"Another time." She wiped her nose with the back of her hand.

"I'm always here, you know that."

"At least you came home."

I smiled at her. "I did. And I'm glad I did."

Her arms were warm around my neck as she hugged me. "At least one of us got our happily ever after," she whispered against me. It felt like her mouth was drawn up into a smile, but it could have been a grimace.

"It's only been a few days," I said. "Not quite the fairy-tale ending, not yet."

And then Andreas came back up from the basement, carrying another bag of badly wrapped gifts and a pillow, and all I could do was hug her.

Chapter Twelve
Thomas

I STARTLED AS the door banged shut, and the voices suddenly went silent, leaving the noise from the TV a little too loud.

"What happened?" I asked. We'd been quietly watching TV, and I'd probably fallen asleep with my wine glass in my hand.

"Who's singing?" Frank asked, pointing at some dude wailing on the screen.

"Adrian something. Never heard of him."

"No wonder. It's not like you ever listen to opera." He laughed, his forehead scrunching as he muttered something to himself.

"What happened?" I asked again, turning towards Lilly, Lottie and Maria standing around the dinner table, looking kind of guilty.

"Andreas and Fredrik went out," Maria said.

"Okay."

"Did you say they were a cute couple because they were gay?" Frank demanded.

"It was just a joke," Lottie said.

"I didn't mean it," Lilly added.

"I said it was a generalisation," Maria protested.

"Yes, indeed." Frank sighed and straightened up. "Kiddos, listen. I honestly think the jokes are old now. Give the boys a break. It's enough having to deal with...what they're dealing with. Cut them some slack."

"We don't need any more drama in the house," I added.

"No, no more drama," Frank agreed. "And not because it's discriminating or homophobic or hate speech, but because it's a hurtful generalisation, and believe me, the boys will hear enough of that in their lives."

I swallowed. I knew what he meant. Life was usually fine. We'd had no major episodes in the homophobia department, but the small comments had always been there, in the open and in our minds, from teachers doubting our skills with the kids, strangers telling the kids to "go tell their mum," to people assuming things about us and our lives. I guess straight couples also got the same kind of generalising comments, and single parents and low-income families and people of colour, and sometimes they'd probably felt it was nothing more than a careless comment.

That didn't make our feelings less valid or the comments less frustrating. It just made me feel like a failure or that we'd made a wrong choice in having kids. I had an urgent need to hug Fredrik and Maria and tell them I loved them, that they were the best things in my life, besides Frank, but then I remembered Fredrik wasn't here and Maria was looking guilty as charged.

"Just…just mind your words," Frank said, frowning again, but his mind seemed to be elsewhere as he turned towards the TV again, then pulled out his phone to check something.

Once again, I was restless. I'd been stressing a lot recently, organising Christmas, planning meals and shopping for nine on top of Frank's appointments and the nurses who came and went like they lived here. The food had been the easiest part, since we had the same meals every Christmas, pork ribs for Christmas Eve, like Frank's family always had, with a vegetarian option for those who didn't eat meat, which had been anything from one to six people over the years. I think I was the only one who'd never opted for the vegetarian course, partly because I liked pork ribs and partly because I was stubborn and didn't want to give them pleasure of being right when they said the vegan Christmas steak was as good as my own fatty overcooked ribs. I could happily eat vegetarian any other day of the year, just not on Christmas Eve.

But that wasn't the only meal to shop for. We'd always invited all our family for lunch on Christmas Day, but the way life worked, the numbers had steadily dwindled. It was just us now and sometimes my uncle Kåre, but not this year. This year was about us, our family being together. Lunch was easy, just a big breakfast, and it was still early enough during the holiday week that the kids hopefully hadn't eaten all the food yet. They also ate less now than they had when they were younger.

We were having salmon on Boxing day, and my family had always had a rack of lamb during Christmas, so I'd insisted on that tradition, mostly for me, with a vegan nut roast on the side. I'd remembered to get candles for the family graves, and we'd bought wreaths at the market earlier. I'd got everything done, remembered everyone that needed to be remembered. I'd even lit a candle for Bella, who was still alive and well in the many books and films proudly stacked on the shelf, next to a remastered photograph the production team had given us. It seemed like years ago now, which it actually had been—a tumultuous period of our lives that had been exciting and new. Until things had faded. The income was a lovely reminder, though. Bella still brought in her audience. Hers was a life that had in no way been wasted, instead bringing so many people joy. She'd been a force, and she'd lived hard and fast, for nobody but herself. She still did, in a way.

Just like that, my mind went back to breakfasts and lunches for all nine of us. There were piles of leftovers to manage, organising the fridges, and the freezer was once again a mess. It wasn't a task to share, either; we'd decided a long time ago that it was better that one of us did the planning and shopping and storing, and the others shared the bill. That didn't stop Gabe from constantly cleaning out and rearranging the fridge, and I'd honestly forgotten when we learned to manage these Christmases, but the learning had certainly happened the hard way and had probably involved over-filling the fridge, things going off and a lot of food we couldn't store and an unhealthy amount of yelling. But we were all still married and still here, so I guess we figured things out somehow.

I'd been in charge of buying the main ingredients for the upcoming dinners yesterday, and we'd had a huge delivery of the other groceries today, and I'd basically felt like a manager of a small food store or a personal shopping assistant unpacking and putting away all the stuff. It looked like something we'd never finish, but I knew we'd be out of food again before New Year's Eve, and then Frank would be on the meal delivery site ordering more and I'd be down the supermarket before breakfast in a frenzy of disorganised chaos.

Right now, I wanted to get moving, not just between the fridge and the boxes on the bench but to go outside, walk, stretch my legs and get some air.

It was something we'd always done, almost every night. It was a long-gone luxury, but still...

"Frank, fancy going for a walk?" I asked.

"Absolutely!" he replied as Gabriel got up and gave him a hand.

I moaned as I stood up. "My legs are at the point of cramping up. I've been playing housekeeper all day."

"Housekeeper? You? Who's been cooking?"

"Who's been planning and organising every meal for the next week?"

"Sure." He laughed at me, the glittering blue eyes I fell in love with ages ago. "Are you guilt tripping me again? Mr *I've done it all*?"

"Oh, shush, Frank," Gabriel mocked. "Let him brag. We'll show off later when he sees our excellent marinade. And that nut roast is the best we've ever made."

I loved that Gabriel was here. He lifted Frank's mood no end—and also told him off when he did too much because Frank was not always good for himself. That was a lesson we'd all learned.

In his defence, we'd been so much better for each other over the past years. Less stress, more love. I was finally back doing only research again; Frank had done some freelance work as a producer at NRK and had never had to return to crappy cinema ads or commercial segments. The boost to his confidence had been immense, even though he hadn't worked at all over the last year. We didn't need him to. It wasn't even on the cards anymore.

We put on our coats and went outside. It had been snowing a bit, but two sets of footsteps leading from the door were clearly visible. Two pairs of size forty-four shoes, a foot apart, walking together.

"I know where they are." I smiled. "Let's go somewhere else."

Taking walks was no longer an option, so we did this instead. Just got in the car, the blanket from the back carefully placed over Frank's legs. Then I rolled slowly along the silent road, happy to see nobody else out, no people, no cars, our tyres making fresh tracks before we turned left down to the park. I'd turn off the engine as we reached the water's edge.

It was a cosy night, cold and snowy, filling me with Christmas cheer. The lake was frozen over, the ice glittering in the half moon's light. We'd moved to this once modern residential area before the kids were born, a decent house on a hill above Oslo with too many trees to have a proper view, but it was lush and green, and we'd called this home ever since. This park, with its small gravelly beach and the trees, held too many memories to mention, and now it was just the two of us here, me still with the dry taste of wine in my mouth, Frank's breaths too shallow for my liking.

"You okay?" he asked, letting out a little puff.

"Yeah. Only had a sip of wine. I'm good to drive if you need me to."

"That's what ambulance services are for, babe," he replied dryly. "You can have a drink. It's Christmas, and fuck you if you think I'm going anywhere at Christmas. That would be bloody cruel."

"Don't." We'd talked about this, made simple plans for if the worst came to the worst. I hated it and wouldn't let it happen. Not ever. Fuck everything.

"I'm fine," he reassured me. "Super tired, but my head is good. It's exactly what I wanted. I was hoping the boys would sort themselves out, and the girls are happy. Maria is running around full of energy, and you're here. What else could I ask for?"

"Not much," I agreed. Things had panned out pretty well. No major arguments, nothing to burst the little bubble of normality I'd so desperately tried to create.

The view from here was amazing all year round, and we'd often walked this way in the evenings with the kids. We used to go sledging along these paths in the winter. There was a small patch of forest as well, and the view from there was even better, but with all the snow over the past days, it wasn't accessible by car.

We settled in where we were instead, and I helped Frank out so he could sit on the green bench not far from the road, the golden glow from the streetlights pouring over it. We'd put on warm coats and scarves and mittens when we left; he had heavy boots and I had our massive seat cushion that I laid down before letting Frank take a seat. The cushion was as much for me as for Frank's fragile legs: neither of us wanted to spend the next fifteen minutes feeling the snow slowly soaking through our jeans.

I traced his fingers, down to the calluses on his palms, over his joints, along his tendons, back up to his rounded fingertips and smooth nails. I thought about what these hands had done, where they'd been, the art they'd made, the pleasure, the joy. No pain, because the pain wasn't in his hands, not even when he'd tried to push me away. I lifted them towards my lips and kissed his fingers, one by one, looking up at him across our joined hands. He filled me with so much joy, this man, filled my heart and mind and all of me with all of him.

Taking Frank's gloved hand in mine, I rested my head on his shoulder, and we sat there quietly, enjoying the view, the golden shine over the city, a burning haze in the cold evening, the downtown lights reflecting in the fog lying like a cover over the city centre. I took off my gloves and pulled Frank's off as well so I could feel his skin against mine despite the cold.

He reached up to stroke my chin. "You're a sappy, sentimental twat."

Oh, well. He was making me sappy. He could see that, too, chuckling as he watched me, lifting his other hand towards my eye, drying a tear with his cold glove. I shrugged and said nothing, but my lips curled into a little smile, one that I wanted to hide because he would always tease me, but I couldn't so I braced myself, anticipating a fight.

But there was no fight. He bent down to kiss me, tenderly, softly, as silent as the hill around us, just our breaths could be heard, and only just.

I nudged my nose against his. "Hey, I love you," I whispered. I didn't know why I couldn't say it louder. It wasn't something I wanted to hide and felt like something I should have shouted all over the winter sky.

He put his arms around me and pulled me closer as if he wanted me to warm him from the inside, and I did my best, trying to be his personal heater right now, hanging on to him as hard as I could.

Suddenly the sky buzzed with colours. Green and violet shades coming out of nowhere, promptly filling the entire horizon above the city. We sat there, amazed by the view. It wasn't often we saw the northern lights like this here, this far south, and definitely not all above us like now.

"What about those northern lights?" I asked against his cold coat. "Did you order them just for me?"

I could feel him smile behind my head. "Nah. I was planning on taking you out here and making you see stars."

"Silly." I laughed, nudging him with my elbow. "If you're not careful, I'll make you see stars. Just not here, I think."

"Not here?" He pretended to unzip his fly.

"Well, sure, if you want to. It might keep you warm."

"I'm hot enough, I think. But you might have to heat me up again when we get home. Those stars sound very tempting."

"Ohhh, that's a very grown-up thing to suggest."

"I don't want you sucking my dick in public in the view of at least five houses where our kids' schoolmates grew up."

I chuckled again. It was a joke but a comfortable one. Both of us knew there would be no stars for either of us, sex no longer being something we could comfortably handle.

"I wonder where the boys are," he mused.

"They're in the forest, no doubt snogging against that rock, hopefully decent. Deciding how to plan out the future."

"Ah, of course. And definitely not getting off and doing unmentionable things in the forest."

"Like getting their feet cold."

He laughed. I loved hearing him laugh. "Hopefully, they have enough common sense to not make themselves all cold and wet. There's a lot of snow up there."

"Fredrik is our son," I pointed out. "How would you rate him on a common-sense scale?"

"Umm... Is biology or the environment the stronger influence, again?"

"Biology."

"Then...a six?"

"Six? On a one to six scale, I presume?"

"Ten."

"Bah humbug." I laughed. "Then it's a nine. He's like me."

"So a six then."

"Ten."

"Six."

"You're so dumb."

"Idiot." He was shaking behind my back while holding me tight around my chest and upper arms, awkwardly hugging me on a bench in the middle of the night as the sky burned bright above us.

"At least biology is stronger than environment," I countered. "If not, he wouldn't even reach the upper half in common sense. You have none, honey."

"What!"

"Nah."

I thought about all the things he'd done—those art projects that had covered our entire street, over-ambitious Christmas dinners, painting our very sturdy family SUV with fluorescent flames, signing up for street-dancing classes on a dare, just to prove a point, forcing Fredrik to learn to knit, in revenge for mocking his moves, and, of course, the fact that he still had highlights streaked through his grey hair in a futile attempt at not looking 'old'.

Soon after, the aurora began to fade, which was as well. We were both freezing. On the way home, Frank brought up Fredrik again.

"I think he's better now. I was in doubt for a while, but I think pushing him into coming home was a good idea."

"He's a bit like you, you know. Needs someone to steer him."

He smiled. "Looks who's talking!"

"And I think Andreas is good for him," I said, putting on my serious face. "He needs someone to be with, and for. He's not made to be alone. He doesn't cope well when he doesn't have someone around to ground him or to make him fly or swim. He'll just fall and fall without any opposite forces exerted on him."

"You don't think it's too much for him? Too much responsibility, too much to handle?"

"Too much? Andreas is a pretty well-functioning young man. It's not like Fredrik needs to watch over him."

"No, not that." He sighed. "I don't think Andreas would cope if they broke up again."

"Funny. That's what Bruno said, too."

"I guess we could see that coming."

"Then you should know Fredrik well enough to know that when he jumps into something, he finishes. He toes the line."

"He quit medicine," he reminded me.

"Well, he was young then. And ambitious. Top grades from school, thinking he was expected to use those grades for the most sought-after studies, too. And pathology is really icky." I shrugged, thinking about brains and blood and gore. "Once he got settled into physics, he ran with it."

"Even if it wasn't the right choice?"

"I think it was always the right choice," I protested. "Just not the right people around him. He didn't get the encouragement he needed, or the support. Or not from the right people, at least. We messed up there. Perhaps we shouldn't have given him all the freedom to do what he wanted, because I'm still not sure moving to the States was the right thing for him."

"It was," Frank said. "He grew up, got some good experiences and paved his own path in life, which has brought him back here. Back to the people who love him. I don't think that can ever be classed as a mistake."

"You're probably right," I agreed, reluctantly. Still didn't mean things didn't hurt. Because when my kids hurt, I hurt. And when Frank hurt, I practically bled. I always had.

"What do you think he will do now?" Frank asked.

"Honestly? I think he'll go to Andreas and stay with him, not caring about whether he has a job or a proper place to live, as long as he has Andreas."

"So Gabriel and Bruno will get two for the price of one, then?"

I chuckled. I honestly couldn't imagine Fredrik staying permanently in their flat. He valued his privacy too much, and having the girls around twenty-four seven would make him twitchy. I loved the girls, but they made me break out in anxious sweats sometimes.

We parked the car on our drive, and I once again let out a breath of relief. The new snow had covered everything, highlighting the many strings of lights, the beautiful wreaths, Christmas trees on the inside, a calm mood lying everywhere. The holidays were truly here.

I opened the car door, then suddenly stopped in my tracks and looked at Frank. "Hey, that Christmas ornament..."

Frank laughed a touch hysterically, as if he didn't need a second to understand what I was asking about. "Yes?"

"Was that...?"

"Was that what?"

"Was it the vibrator we bought in Copenhagen that summer?"

He chuckled again. "Yes. The one that never worked. I found it the other day."

"So you...made it into an ornament?"

"Yup. I painted it green and dipped it in glitter. In my own private little Christmas workshop."

"For fuck's sake, Frank."

"It was funny. It *is* funny. And it's very me."

"It is indeed. Very creative."

"You didn't like it?"

"No!" I laughed. "We have a sex toy hanging on our Christmas tree!"

"Like anyone cares. It made you laugh, and that's all I wanted. Good stuff. Job done."

"Now I'm worried what I'll find under the tree tomorrow."

"You don't want to know." He grinned. "I could have made it more creative if I'd had more time."

"You're creative enough for both of us." I sighed. "Just as long as you know that you will be getting exactly what you wrote down on your wish list. There will be no surprises."

"Just the way I like it." He yawned. "Now help me out of this damn car so I can go lie down."

If the house was beautiful on the outside, the inside was surprisingly silent and clean. The dinner table was set for tomorrow, white plates, crystal glasses, silverware, just like always, and napkins on each plate, not a complicated fold, just rolled and decorated with festive ribbons. The Christmas tree sparkling in front of the big windows, the glowing embers in the fireplace giving the room an orange afterglow. I think I heard low voices coming from somewhere in the house, although I wasn't sure who they were or where from.

Frank had found another spurt of energy and came up from the basement carrying a stack of cake tins. "I just remembered where they were. A bit too late, but whatever. Cake tins. Sorted. And by the way, the basement is empty. The bed is deflated and folded, and the duvet is packed away. Looks like we no longer have a guest downstairs."

"Just as well." I grinned. "Let's not check whether we have the guest somewhere else, shall we?"

He sat on the sofa and smiled at me. "Come 'ere," he said, patting the seat next to him. I did as I was told, resting my head on his shoulder. My eyes slid shut as I allowed myself to relax, relishing the heat from him, his breath, the gentle movement of his fingers on my shoulder, his hair tickling my neck. My man.

"You know, everything will be all right in the end," he whispered.

I didn't answer that because I didn't want to think like that. So I said nothing.

We both leaned into each other, and all was well.

Chapter Thirteen
Andreas

I looked at him. Watched him. Drank him in with my eyes, over and over again, but it always felt rushed, like if I accidentally looked away, it would be all over.

The truth was, I was terrified of losing him again, this man in my arms, his head heavy on my chest, his arm curled around my neck, his breathing soft and warm against my skin. My Freddie.

Thinking back, I was always fascinated with him, probably from the first time I saw him. He had this air of cool around him, a confidence I envied from a kid younger than myself, because at seventeen, I'd considered myself a grown-up. I'd been kissed and messed around with girls. Felt a boob through a bra. Played with the hem of someone's knickers. Her name was Leona and she was very cute, but yeah. I could admit it to myself now. She hadn't been Freddie.

Neither had any of the boys been—those boys my Papi had talked about. I'd never thought about them like that, and it made sense. I'd always been possessive over my friends, but with Freddie, I think I'd gone into overdrive. Perhaps I'd even scared him away before I'd intentionally pushed him. I wasn't always easy to deal with. I knew that.

Nobody was like him or had ever been, with the little kink in his nose, his strong eyebrows and impossibly long eyelashes. The sharp line of his jaw and his soft skin. His lips that just begged to be kissed.

Talk about making someone feel inadequate. I'd happily licked the lines of his stomach, and there were definitely some muscles hanging around there. Firm, defined arms and pecs to die for. He was even more gorgeous now, more than he'd ever been as a fresh-faced teen. Now he was fit. Beautiful. Mine.

I might have been the fool here and my Vati was absolutely right. I needed to own this. Carry him. Let him in so he could carry me too. Vati had used all those posh emotional words to describe it, while he might be right, I knew what I needed. Perhaps I knew what Freddie needed too.

"I love you," I whispered into his hair. It didn't matter that he didn't say it back because I knew he loved me. I could see it in the way he looked at me, and thus I was laying here smiling, kissing his still-damp hair, the long strands he had so effortlessly bundled into a little man bun. Mine was short and straggly, my fringe once again covering my eyes. I'd had it cut before Christmas, but it grew like out-of-control weeds, ruining any attempt at looking civilised within days.

I thought back to the first time I'd kissed him…well, it hadn't involved magic or butterflies or stars and sparkling rainbows. It had simply been a kiss, lips against lips, muffled giggles and cheeks flushed with embarrassment, his fingers fisting my T-shirt over my heart, my own hand lying limp on his hip.

We'd laughed, and I had fully expected him to roll away from me, ending what had been a stupid idea in the first place. But he hadn't. He'd grabbed my hand and held on as he'd launched that mouth of his over mine, tasted me, licked me and crawled on top of me with all the gusto of a perma-horny sixteen-year-old. He hadn't known what he was doing, but his enthusiasm had been contagious, and I think I just lost the plot, there and then. We both lost some clothes, the mosquitoes buzzing around at the top of the tent suddenly having a feast of skin at their mercy. We hadn't noticed. Nothing had mattered but the two of us, our lips, our hands.

We hadn't been able to look at each other afterwards. I'd turned over, pretending to go to sleep. He'd giggled and kicked me with his cold feet and crawled into the sleeping bag with me, stretching it until the seams felt like they were going to burst.

My chest jumped with held-back laughter thinking about it now, the two of us, stupid children playing at being all grown up.

Then I'd hurt him, over and over again, this kid who idolised me and hung onto my every word, who wouldn't stop telling me that he loved me and would hold me and make the world around us disappear.

He'd confused me for years, made me doubt everything. I was not gay. I was not like my fathers. I was not confused. I was me, and I was perfectly normal.

Bullshit.

I knew that now. I had no idea how genetics worked or if conditioning was a thing, and to be honest it was all just fucking ridiculous. I fell in love with this boy with his golden locks and little dimples, and that was it. Nobody else lived up to my stupid ideals, ever again. However beautiful and pretty and smooth other people were, talking to me and tricking my stupid ego into thinking I had found someone who could make me feel better about myself. All they needed to do was kiss me and my head would nosedive into the gutter. They weren't him. They didn't taste right, didn't move right, and they never smelt anywhere as good as the man in my arms. I breathed him in, of course I did. Buried my face in his curls and wiggled my nose around.

"Too tired," he whispered and curled into me tighter. Then he rolled over and let me spoon him again, my nose in his neck, my lips on his skin, my cock jerking as my hips settled against his arse.

I'd always let him fuck me. He took my virginity, and I took his an hour later. Then I let him do me again, loving the feel of him inside me. Yes, of course it fucking hurt, but I loved the sounds he made, the strength of him holding me down, the way he lost control just before he exploded into the condom, his chest flushed red and his cheeks glowing, his face a mix of ecstasy and pure embarrassment. He was funny. He made me laugh. He made me feel like I was the king of the world.

So, I would let him fuck me. Again and again. Sometimes he would ask, and sometimes I would indulge him in a little bit of bottoming, but I was still always happiest when he was inside me. I'd said it before: he grounded me, and fuck, there was nowhere I felt more grounded than when he was fucking the living daylights out of me and his cock would swell and—

"I want to fuck you, baby," I whispered into his neck.

"You can do whatever you want to me," he whispered back.

Which, of course, brought tears to my over emotional twat-feature eyeballs. Fucking hell. I was turning into my dads. You told either of them that you loved them and they'd go all emo, tears and hugs and shit all over the place.

I reached over and said a silent prayer of thanks to Thomas, god of preparations and purchaser of the finest lube sachets this side of the Fjord. And condoms. Big ones. Neither of us was under-equipped in the cock department. How on earth Thomas knew this was a mystery to me. Well. I suppose it wasn't. Lilly did draw a size chart once.

I coated my fingers in lube, throwing the wrapper over my shoulder as I positioned myself under the duvet, keeping him on his side facing away from me, his knees already curled up, just waiting, his body trembling in anticipation. He had the most stunning backside. A firm, rounded butt. The tightest little hole in the world. Well, what did I know? I'd only ever been inside this one because none of the others the world had offered up to me compared.

I stroked my fingers around his opening, coating his skin in silky fluid before working my middle finger inside of him. I'd never quite figured out if I was doing this right, always too ashamed to google it or ask. Freddie had no such qualms. He researched and watched instructional videos while I squirmed and hid behind a pillow. He could have me loose and begging for him within minutes, while I still needed a bit of trial and error to get Freddie in the mood, get him relaxed enough so a second finger could join the first. Lots of kissing and a bit of dirty talk because he secretly loved it.

"Did you miss my cock?" I asked. Lame, I knew, but it made him giggle.

"Fuck you," he said.

"Come on, baby. Be a good boy, open up your hole for my fingers," I grunted, hoping to sound like some fucked-up porno daddy.

I'd never watched any gay pornos and certainly had no idea how to sound like a big, hairy, porno daddy. (Lies. All of it.) But I was no fucking bear-like creature, and he was not a twinky-looking boy, who was probably some thirty-six-year-old estate agent in real life, doing a bit of gay-for-pay. I had not watched any of that crap. Ever.

He made some kind of gurgling noise against the wall, which I knew was a good sign.

"Come on, just relax and let me get inside that tight hole. Gonna make you beg for my cock, babe. Because you want it, don't you? My big fat cock instead of my fingers. Would that be good? My big fat cock splitting—"

"Fucking hell, Andreas." He rolled over and dragged me down so he could kiss me while my fingers slid out of him and I ended up being manhandled until I was flat against the bedroom wall with his rock-hard cock poking me in the stomach.

"You watch too much damn porn," he muttered into my mouth. "Now, does Daddy have to show you how to do this properly?"

"Not my Daddy," I said, trying to keep my voice stern when all I wanted to do was to burst into laughter.

"I'll show you who's the Daddy," he growled and put his mouth back on mine. It was filthy, the kiss he dished out, all slow licks and little sighs and grunts and his cock sliding against my stomach as he went all caveman on me again. In a second, I was flat on my back with him straddling my stomach, and my fingers were finally back against his hole while he was kind of jerking himself off in my face and yup. It was hot. Hot enough that my cock was ready to burst down there.

"Kiss..." I slurred.

"Open your mouth," he hissed at me, moving closer and leaning over so the tip of his cock painted my lips with wetness.

I kissed his foreskin as my head kind of spun. He could pretend he was the Daddy all he wanted, but I could still tease. I knew what made him tick.

"Open your goddamn mouth and suck my dick." He rolled his hips again, getting a second finger inside of him. I could go deeper like this with his cock sinking into my mouth.

"Good boy," his filthy mouth said. "Suck me. That's it, take it deep, baby. All the way back."

I gagged a little. Yup. I was out of practice, not having done this for years since... Since forever.

"Just relax, babe, let me all the way in. Yeah. That's it."

Fuck, he was in a filthy, dirty mood. Too tired, my arse. My eyes were watering at the intrusion, his cock making me cough and splutter as he pulled out and looked down at me.

"Look at me," he whispered.

I nodded, swallowing excess spit as I scissored my fingers hard inside of him, making him gasp for breath as his body shivered above me.

"Again?" I teased, my voice a little raspy. I didn't even have to put it on.

"Fuck." He groaned as I pressed a third finger against his opening. He could take it. I knew he could.

"Are you going to be good?" I asked. "Dirty bastard, fucking my throat like that."

"You love it," he muttered and filled my mouth again. His cock sliding home as I greedily took him, trying to suck and relax as my body spasmed with my gag reflex going off like crazy. My body moved underneath him, my cock leaking liquid that I could feel dripping against my stomach, my fingers fucking his arse as hard as I could muster as my feet kicked the bedposts and my head started to swim. I was so close, and I was going to come if he kept this up. He always made me all embarrassed and horny and ridiculous, usually coming well before I was supposed to.

"Need to fuck you now," I mumbled as he pulled his dick out of my mouth, walking backwards on his knees until I could feel his hole against the tip of my cock. "Condom," I whispered.

"Don't want to," he whispered back, his eyes staring me down. "It's only ever going to be you, and I was tested a few weeks back."

"What? You want...I mean. No condoms?"

"No condoms, Andreas." He bent down and kissed my lips. "It's only been a few days, but I mean it. I can't do casual with you. I am serious about this, one hundred percent. It's you and me now, all the time, forever. Can you deal with that?"

"I can deal with that," I whispered, and my traitorous eyes were welling up again. "I love you. Fucking hell, I love you so much it hurts."

"I know," he whispered and sank his arse down over the tip of my cock.

It had always felt weird. Warm, tight and frightening and wonderful all wrapped up into one as I squeezed my eyes shut and my mouth did some kind of *Ohhhh!* thing. I could smell him, the distinct scent of sex and sweat and arousal and body fluids and oh fuck. Oh fuckety-fuck.

"Oh yeah." He moaned as he took the last of me inside of his body and his arse came to a rest against my balls. "Oh hell. Oh fucking fuck."

"What?" I giggled because he was...he was just *something*.

"You feel amazing. Warm. I love it. So much better than with all that latex."

I didn't know how he could still speak in perfect sentences when I could barely get my brain into gear. The sensations overwhelmed me as he started to move, just small movements, up and down, cold air hitting my cock then warm wet heat, and friction. Delicious friction as every part of my body erupted in goosebumps and my cheeks burned and my brain was full of static and my mouth was making sounds again.

"Just come," he grunted. "Don't hold back. Just do it. Fill me up. I want you to come inside of me, all of it. The full monty."

"If you talk dirty to me like that, you will…" I didn't get any more words out before I shot my load and most of my brain it seemed, as my hips arched off the bed with him still riding me, and his hands were suddenly around my face and his lips were back on mine, his cock jerking between our bodies as he kissed me and rutted against me in some kind of desperate dance of need. My softening cock slid out of him.

"Take it. Take what you need," I whispered into his neck as he moaned out loud.

"Need inside of you," he replied. I was already reaching for the lube.

He grabbed it off me, leaning on his elbows at first, then rising up to expose his gorgeous self to me, all flushed and his hair damp by his temples, his nipples tight buds of brown and his chest rising and falling like he'd been running.

"Don't prep me, just go for it," I hissed. Because. Well. I needed it. Wanted it. I wanted to feel him—wanted to feel everything—and I was already too sensitive everywhere to be able to handle anything but.

"Don't want to hurt you," he muttered as his hand covered his length in lube.

"You won't. You would never hurt me," I said and lifted my knees up to my chest.

He still prepped me, just the bare minimum until I was shouting for him to fuck me or I would die from the need for him to fuck me. Even then, he was laughing and complaining that my come was running down his leg. I threatened him with years of washing sheets every day because no condoms was a messy business. I knew because my Papi had told me all the facts of life when I was maybe eighteen and he'd had to wash my soiled sheets…again. I blamed it on Freddie. He probably blamed it on me because Papi had spoken to him too. Man to Man.

Freddie kissed me and quietly whispered that he loved me. I told him I loved him back, over and over again, not even taking his words in. I wanted to hear it again.

He hid his face in my neck, and I told him it was okay, that I would love him enough for the two of us.

He said he didn't believe me. I threatened to shout it from the rooftops. Then there was banging on the ceiling from above, and the Christmas carols were turned up to some new ridiculous volume in Maria's room, and I couldn't stop smiling.

I loved him, and I wanted the world to know.

Despite one of the girls shouting, "Shut the fuck up and stop shagging," from the hallway.

It didn't matter. I loved him.

Chapter Fourteen
Frank

CHRISTMAS EVE HAD been nice so far. I'd woken up with Thomas, our feet tangled and his arm slung across me. His crotch was almost glued to my ass, nothing between us. He fit so well there, his dick into my cleft, yet where my own dick would once have been growing, the damn chemicals I was pumping through my body had put a swift end to my sex drive. Not that I had any energy or strength for something like that, but still. These mornings were the closest thing to sex I got these days, and all in all, they were comforting, especially the ones where I would slowly wake up and imagine that this was my life. Where my body shut the hell up and just let me live.

Then the magic was lost when I realised I really, really had to pee, and my head was throbbing so I needed water and perhaps some painkillers. I may have grown weak. Also Thomas and I *may* have drunk all the remaining gluhwein last night, and the jug *may* have been a bit bigger than I'd realised. We *may* have been a bit unsteady as we went to bed. And I was not supposed to have any alcohol. Well, it was Christmas and I truly had stopped caring.

Luckily, we were sleeping on the ground floor, not far from the living room. Sometimes it was not much of a perk, like when three young ladies came home drunk at four in the morning, high on dancing and kebabs and too much booze and inevitably bumped into all the kitchen cupboards in their quest for more food to fix the sugar cravings. But sometimes universal design was fine, like when you only had to walk a few metres to your bedroom door and the bathroom was on the way and everything was clean and tidy and well known and there was nothing to stumble over.

I wondered if we'd tidied up after us or if the gluhwein leftovers were still oozing their sweet, alcoholic smell on the table. I was pretty sure the sofa cushions were straight, though. I had a vivid memory of a giggling Thomas insisting on fluffing every pillow on our corner sofa to perfection before going to bed, despite me trying my very best to pull him with me. Sometimes he was very cute, my Thomas. Well, most of the time, actually, but sometimes particularly so.

Not even my promise of an imaginary blow job if he'd just come put me to bed *now* could have stopped him from continuing the fluff job, but he still smiled and gave me a dirty kiss once we finally got to bed. He threatened to pinch my ribs in his sleep if I didn't sleep naked, so in the end I'd obeyed. Hence now I was all wobbly on my feet, trying to grab both underwear and a top before stumbling out into the living room, making my way over to the bathroom.

My balance wasn't always on point, so I sat down to do my business, leaning over on my elbows and wondering if the room could please stop spinning, just for a second so I could think. It wasn't the alcohol; it was just my body these days, so no elegance there, and suddenly all I wanted was to be back in bed on my own, allowing my body to rest instead of my husband trying to get in some advanced cuddling.

I missed having the strength to satisfy him. I wanted to taste him, his warm dick, the velvety soft skin along the hard shaft, his shivers when I drew my tongue back and forth under the head, when I swallowed him as far back as I could, played with his balls in my palm, a finger, then his movements got faster and heavier against my mouth. I missed the way his face would change when everything tilted. I remembered his eyes on mine, a flash of fear, excitement, relief, pure joy.

I'd always look up at his face as he came. Lying back, his eyes would shut and he'd push his head into the pillow while trying to hold on to something, the sheets, his hair, his nipples, my hair, trying not to push too hard at my head, then his hips would thrust off the mattress as he came. He'd shoot at my throat with his entire body, and suddenly he'd open his eyes and look at me, a dark deep stare that always pulled me in wherever I was and in whatever state I was in. Always there, always mine.

"Did you make coffee?" I barely heard the words from under the duvet when I got back to the room. The air had a whiff of musk and sweat and alcohol, memories hanging in the air.

"No, but I brought water and painkillers."

"I'm not a wimp. I want coffee," he complained.

I chuckled and returned to the kitchen to make us coffee. I left the water and the paracetamol, though, and they were gone when I got back a few minutes later. I'd used Italian espresso beans in our double Jura, the light-brown crema perfect on top of the black liquid. Bruno would have been proud of me.

"Thank you." The relief was obvious in his face when he got his cup. He needed his coffee, my Thomas. As did I, for the record; we were completely compatible there. It was just that I had no appetite these days. Food made me nauseous. I struggled with coffee. Water made me retch. I lived on juice, and that made my stomach go on strike, bombarding my poor body with the taste of acid.

I crawled back into bed, and Thomas had stuffed the pillows just the way I needed them to be so I could half sit up and try to enjoy my own cup. I could smell it, but the thought of drinking it made my stomach hurt.

"Merry Christmas," he said softly. "Are you ready for today?"

I nodded. I was as ready as I could be. Food ready, recipes ready, table set, dishes planned. I even had a schedule, although we all knew it would fail and we'd never have dinner on time.

"How are you feeling?" His voice was a low hum against my skin, and he carefully placed his hand on my chest as if it was ready to hold me no matter what. I knew he always was.

I had to ponder a bit to get to the right answer. I had felt okay recently, not euphoric and high, despite my baking frenzies and projects in bits and pieces all over the place, and I'd been exhausted because my body was trying to kill me. But things had not been awful, my energy levels dropping in an expected way, more as a result of a busy couple of days and as a result of being active, of using my brain and hands. I had spent so much time in bed lately, trying to read, trying to think, trying to fight. I was tired, and I was so sick and tired of being just that.

"I'm fine," I said.

"It's not too much?"

"No. No, I think it's okay."

"Don't overdo yourself," he begged. "You know, there are nine grown-ups here now. You don't have to do everything."

I chuckled. "I know, but I like to cook. I enjoy thinking everything is normal."

"I know," he smiled. "And I like it when you cook. You're sexy in your apron." I heard his smile against my neck as he stole a nibble at my skin.

"Hush, or I'll smack you with the imaginary spatula I've got hidden under the bed." I laughed.

"How come you thought that would make me be quiet?"

"Right, bad move. Hush, or I won't smack you, then."

"Now we're talking."

His arms were warm as they rolled me over against his chest.

So, as usual, I cooked for us. Well, mostly I sat on a chair gasping for breath while Gabe tried to follow my erratic instructions. Then he'd stop and come and sit down opposite me, telling me to calm the fuck down and let him think. In a nice way. And then we'd laugh at the stupidity and surrealness of it all. That kind of made everything all right. Thomas had done the shopping, but none of us trusted him with the cooking. Well, that's what we said, but the truth was, I wanted to pretend that some things in my life were still normal. For Thomas. For the kids. Mostly for myself. Bruno helped me, though. He chopped and sautéed and watched and asked curious questions that made me search on the internet and almost forget the sugar in the pan we were making caramel sauce with. We probably had some store-bought sauce in the cupboard, but we just managed to save it, all while Gabriel had gone outside to have a cry. He tried to hide it, but I knew. Of course I fucking knew. It wasn't easy being the cause of this clusterfuck of a Christmas, but... Fuck.

I made pork ribs as usual, and a wrapped nut roast, as well as all the side dishes—boiled and jacket potatoes, steamed carrots and Brussels sprouts, the heavy sauce made from the fat and juices from the ribs, lingonberry jam from berries we'd picked this autumn, some jellies from the Christmas market, my own dark apple butter, sauerkraut made by Bruno.

Thomas went out for a couple of hours in the early afternoon, while the ribs were roasting, to visit the family graves. Bruno stayed at home to watch the food, Gabriel to keep an eye on me. Lilly and Lottie hung around with Maria; Fredrik and Andreas hung on to each other; I slept. It was that kind of awful sleep where you felt more exhausted than you had before you lay down. The kind of sleep full of terrible dreams with no ending and no beginning, and I woke up in a sweat, shouting words I didn't even understand.

I was exhausted by the time we had dinner. Half an hour 'too late', according to some traditions, but according to our tradition, it was well within limits, and nobody was complaining. They'd watched some terrible Christmas movie while they waited, or at least most of them had, none of them starving by the looks of the empty tins and wrapping paper that littered the living room floor. Fredrik and Andreas had finally reappeared after two rounds of being called to the table, with their ties askew and tousled hair. Everyone was happy with the food, tender ribs with crispy rind, and the nut roast was perfectly moist. They were all stuffed afterwards, and we had plenty of leftovers for our Christmas Day lunch. Exactly as it should be. I'd managed a mouthful and been sick in the kitchen sink. I'd made it into a joke. Nobody had laughed.

The living room was decorated as it usually was—a mix of decorations, no theme, no plan. I loved red amaryllis, so we had plenty of those, some spruce on the table, stuff the kids had made, things we had bought and candles, loads of candles, throwing a warm mood over the room and warming the room in general.

After dinner, we had coffee and biscuits and cakes and desserts, cream with cloudberries and krumkake, and risalamande with cherry sauce. Bruno had brought both panettone and stollen, both made from family recipes, filled with his own delicious candied citrus peel instead of the chemical-tasting store-bought one. The man kept pretending he couldn't cook, but I knew his secrets, and I'd always laugh, tapping my nose. Then he'd blush. The idiot.

There were gifts, loads of them, most of them kind of useful even for an old married couple with grown-up kids. Sweaters, shirts, socks, kind of dull, but Thomas and Bruno especially seemed to appreciate the efforts to dress them for the next year, I thought. Their matching shirts and ties were a highlight and made me laugh. There were drinks, wine and sweet liqueurs and whisky and more wine. And coffee, of course, bags of locally roasted beans, new gadgets. I had got a new AeroPress for Thomas, and he looked kind of perplexed as he opened it before handing me my gift—of course one for me. Apparently, we were both good at gifts—and remembering things we'd put on our lists. Andreas had gifted Fredrik socks, and Fredrik had gifted Andreas an almost identical pair. The two of them in hysterics made my day, as they'd both cursed their stupidity.

Now the house was finally calm and quiet. The girls had cleared up after dinner, all leftovers were boxed and cooled as per my instructions, ready for tomorrow's lunch, and some would just disappear. That was what happened with independent kids in the house: they helped themselves, to say the least. Lottie had come in and given me a full report in bed, ticking off my list on where to put things and bringing me a small plate of treats.

"You don't need to eat them, Uncle Frank," she said, putting the plate next to me on the bedside table, knocking off a bunch of pill boxes in the process. "But perhaps they would do you more good than your massive haul of drugs here."

"My massive haul of drugs is keeping me alive, thank you very much," I pretend-huffed, and she laughed.

"You're like the worst kind of dealer you see in those crime dramas. The kingpin bathing in dollar bills and letting pills run through his fingers."

"I don't know what crime dramas you watch, young lady, but I don't see anyone bathing in dollar bills here."

"You could have done, a few years back when you started getting those royalty cheques."

"Yeah, until you started asking for shoes. What were those shoes you asked for? Lamborghinis?"

"Louboutin's." She smiled. "Stupid, I know. I had no idea. No sense."

"You were a teenager. You weren't supposed to have any sense. Luckily, you do now. I'm really proud of you and Lils. You know that, don't you?"

"I do," she whispered. "And your nurse just parked up on the drive, so do you want me to change your shirt? You have gravy down the front."

"I look like shit, don't I?" I laughed. "Is it that handsome nurse? The one with the side fringe?"

"It is indeed." She grinned. The girl wasn't even blushing. "So let's make a good impression and wear this snazzy jumper here, and I will pretend to be all concerned and caring while you give him shit. I promise not to laugh this time, but it's Christmas. Let's have some fun."

"Lotts?" I said, as she ripped the shirt over my head and threw it in the corner.

"Yes?" She absentmindedly ripped the labels from some piece of clothing I must have been gifted.

"Don't ever change."

"Hell no." She laughed. "I'm going to spend my whole life raising hell, and you'd better be here to watch me."

I wanted to tell her that I would be. That she was my Lottie and would always make me smile. Even when she'd been small, she'd been my little soul mate. She always would be. Whatever happened, I'd always have her back. I wished I could have promised her that, but my words got stuck in my throat and instead I just let her dress me and brush my pathetic strands of hair.

Bruno and Gabriel had gone out for a walk; I suppose it was their turn to feel a bit strangled inside now. It happened to all of us over the holidays, too many people in too little space. But we coped. We all knew that if we needed to take a timeout, no questions would be asked.

So that was Christmas, and now I was here in my bed, running another fever and getting my nightly dose of antibiotic drip or whatever crap they were pumping into my frazzled veins. The nurse was taking my bloods again, and Lottie was chattering away as he quietly blushed at her intrusive questions. I just laughed. I mean, what was I supposed to do? Scold her for her frankness? Maybe I was expected to think the same about Maria and Fredrik, too, but honestly, they grew up years ago and I was kind of glad she was here and not them. The two of them were always interrogating the nursing staff, asking questions that I didn't want to know the answers to, checking levels, reading leaflets, being concerned. I couldn't bear it. I just wanted them here doing normal things. Sitting in bed. Chatting. Laughing. Taking the piss out of me.

I couldn't stop the smile that split my face when I thought about it. Life was good that way. I was happy when surrounded by happy people. I trusted myself now, trusted that I could do good, that I could love and was loved. I'd been one hell of a parent, I knew that. And I loved Thomas, as he loved me. We may have had our quirks and bad moments, but we'd always worked it out, and in the end I think we'd managed quite well. God, I hoped we had.

I must have fallen asleep at some point, as I was startled awake by a creak in the floorboards. *They need to be fixed,* I thought, my head still deep in fog, *or tightened or whatever one does with creaky boards.* But there were light steps across the floor as my eyes finally adjusted to the soft light.

"Hi, Fredrik. I thought you were...er, is there anything I can do for you? Are you okay? Do you need anything?" I tried to sit up and was half on my way to getting whatever he wanted or needed before remembering I was a wreck and would probably fall flat on my face as soon as I tried to stand up. Also, I had a drip in my arm. Note to self: drink the bloody water. Apparently, I was dehydrated and would be on a drip for the night.

"No, Dad, everything is fine. I, eh..." He bit his lower lip and swallowed as if he was nervous. "Can I sit?"

"Sure, son. What's up?" I felt a lump growing in my stomach, a million thoughts rushing through my mind.

He didn't say anything, but then my son had never been a chatterbox. Not like Maria who'd talked non-stop from the minute she'd figured out what her mouth could do. I watched him instead as he bent forward to grab a bottle of water left on the bedside table. His hand trembled slightly and the bottle clunked loudly against the rim of the glass as he poured water into it.

"Your temperature is up again. I can feel it," he said, gently touching my forehead.

"I probably need some more meds then." I sighed, letting Fredrik find the right blister pack and pop the dry-tasting pills in my mouth. I swallowed the water, and he took the glass back, refilling it like a robot.

He was rattled by something. I would even go as far as saying he was upset, but I couldn't read to what degree, if he was distraught or just nervous. It filled me with sorrow that we'd become so distant that I could no longer read my own son, although it was perhaps no wonder with the physical distance we'd had over the past years.

He took a large gulp from the glass, and I lifted my eyebrows to question his actions. I put my hand on his. "Fredrik, what's wrong?"

He stared at my hand on top of his. His eyes fixated on my fingers. It was like our hands had frozen together, although I could feel his shiver under mine.

"Is it Andreas? Where is he?"

He shook his head. "No, no, it's not him. He's in my room. He's fine. We're fine."

Fredrik sighed and finally managed to look at me. His green eyes were dark, the pupils seeming to fill the irises, hiding the rainbow and glitter in them. He'd seemed so happy recently, happy and care-free, as if all his worries had been lifted off his shoulders. Now the darkness was back in his eyes again, making him seem smaller than he was. My boy. My gorgeous, gorgeous boy.

Suddenly the room seemed darker, the shadows creeping closer, and the few candles still burning, well, the flames no longer seemed comforting but instead were almost menacing as I braced myself for whatever he wanted to tell me.

He blew out a long breath before starting to speak.

"Dad, you know when I was younger and you and Thomas explained to me and Maria that you were sick and that your brain hurt and later told us that the illness was called bipolar?" He looked at me full of fear.

I nodded. I hadn't expected that to be the topic bothering him. We'd always tried to be honest with the kids, be it about how they were created and born or about my illness. Life had taught us that such things were not to be hidden, and yes, we'd held some things back but had learnt that the important things should and could never stay hidden in the long run. Hiding meant shame, and if there was one thing we wanted to instil in our kids, it was that having a mental illness was no shame.

I opened my mouth to say something—something about shame and pride and that I hoped he would never be afraid to tell me that he or anyone he loved was sick.

He held up his hand to stop me. "Wait, Dad, let me talk or I'll never say it."

He breathed deeply. His face suddenly seemed too pale and his lips dry and chapped, and he bit them before he continued to speak. "You said you had bipolar and that it meant that sometimes you would be very sad and very tired, and sometimes you would seem very happy and eager." The words were flowing fast, and he looked down again. "I...I never asked you more. I thought it was okay, that it was something we coped with on a daily basis already, so nothing changed after you put a name on it. You were still my dad and that was it."

I felt a warm flash through my body, like hot waves rushing through it, from toes and fingertips through legs and arms to my heart. It warmed me to hear that nothing had changed. I remembered this conversation. It was after a particularly heavy episode. I didn't think the kids saw much of the mania, but they certainly lived through the depression afterwards, with one dad running the show and the other uselessly staying in bed for weeks, missing their school performances and end-of-school picnics and planting an uncertainty about vacations that year. But we had managed to go on holiday as planned, I didn't remember where. I just remembered that we drove there by car. Thomas had driven all the way and I'd been dozing in the passenger seat, trying not to be too obvious about being totally exhausted. And then we had talked to them about the name of the illness, after advice from my therapist. She thought it was important to give them a name for it, make it real. It had been real enough, I realised that now, and that was probably another mistake we'd made.

After that, we'd had every intention of talking more about it, but time flew and the kids didn't ask, not even when we asked them if they had questions, so we let it be, just filled in with more information as it was appropriate over the years.

"You know, I googled it after you told us," he continued. "And the article said that the suicide risk in bipolar patients was much, much higher than for other people."

He was truly pale now. His voice was steady, but there was an edge to it that told me that he was on the verge of breaking. "After that, I was afraid. I feared your depression, any change in your moods, because I thought it could be a mania if you even seemed happy about something simple." He looked into the back corner of the room like he was trying to avoid my gaze. "And then the depression would follow, or something I thought was a depression, maybe you were just tired and wouldn't get up, but I feared you were depressed. Then I started watching everything you did, to make sure you didn't kill yourself. Sometimes I would fake being ill so I could stay at home with you, and I sometimes hated Thomas for not caring enough about you to stay at home. I got obsessed with not leaving you on your own because I thought if we did, you would kill yourself."

I opened my mouth to say something, but no sound came out.

"It was like I could never relax, and I tried to ask Maria, but she just shrugged and never seemed to worry. I couldn't even sleep all night when you were sick. I just wanted to sleep next to you so I could watch you, then maybe I could sleep, but Thomas said you had to rest."

I drew my breath with a sharp sound. I remembered the nights when Fredrik had come in to lie next to me. Sometimes it was okay. Sometimes I'd let him do it for an hour or half an hour in the afternoon, but at night I'd turn my back to him and try to push him off the bed, and if Thomas was there,

I'd whisper good night to Fredrik and let Thomas take him away. We'd even told him off, had conversations about the importance of a good night's sleep.

I thought he'd been going through an annoying phase, constantly disturbing my rest and sleep. It never occurred to me that he was afraid and wanted to watch me.

"And then, years later, I talked to Andreas, and I knew that both his dads were sometimes depressed, but Andreas was never afraid. He just looked at me in surprise when I told him about my fear and said that he didn't think his Papi would do that, and his Vati? No. Never. So why worry? It made me feel so incredibly stupid. But by then, it was just so ingrained in who I was. I spent years being terrified of losing you."

I had no idea what to say, so I just lay there and let my son talk. Let him rip me to shreds with the honesty that was wounding my soul, with every word slipping from his mouth.

"And I really tried to think that you wouldn't want to either, that we were too important to you, that you wanted to stay with us and didn't want us to suffer through a suicide or a suicide attempt. But I had read about it, and I couldn't forget about the despair and the feeling of being worthless and that our lives would be better without you, so I couldn't rule out you doing it."

And right there something shattered inside me.

I thought we'd done right by telling them. I thought we did right by not pushing them to talk, by not forcing anything on them. And maybe we were right, but Fredrik, my Fredrik, the one closest to my soul, had suffered and feared and carried this fear for half a lifetime.

"And now we're here, and I am terrified, Dad. I don't know what to do. How to feel. What to say. Because whatever I fucking do, I can't fix you. I can't make this bloody body of yours heal. Maybe if I'd finished my medicine degree...maybe I could have seen it sooner, noticed shit that we all missed and could have saved you. I know it sounds insane, but my head isn't in a good place now, and I can't even deal. I don't want this. I never wanted this. This is everything I feared, everything I have spent my whole life being terrified of. I can't. I can't deal, Dad."

The shards were falling inside me, scratching my insides. It hurt, stung, burnt, as if someone was cutting me, but it was only me, my soul, my mind, my heart, shattering into pieces, small pieces that could still cut me, slice me, kill me from the inside. My body did what it always did. I turned away because I couldn't bear for him to see me like this, all weak and destroyed with nothing left to soothe those fears. It had come down to this, and there was nothing I could do to change it.

I felt the heat from him against my back, arms around me, his naked face against my neck, tears falling on my back, making a wet spot on the shoulder of the jumper I was wearing. His sobs made me shatter even more. I imagined him making these sounds at my death bed, at my funeral, at my grave, and everything shattered once again.

We lay there, on top of the bed, a man at the edge of life, an empty glass now on the floor, water soaking the carpet, my son's arms around my neck, or perhaps it was the other way around, my son holding me together. Maybe he was the one stopping me from letting everything just fall apart.

There was nothing I could do to change his past. Our past. My mistakes. My stupid, stupid head. But it could have been much, much worse, unbearable, if my life had been spent without him.

Chapter Fifteen
Fredrik

It FELT LIKE I was negotiating a narrow ledge, not quite managing to balance, not sure on which side I would fall, but Andreas was here, and I tried desperately to focus on that, on his arms around me, his body, his smell, his mouth, his lips, his soothing voice.

I wasn't sure how I'd got back to him after I'd completely crushed Dad. I remember crushing my dad. My dad whom I loved, had always loved, would always love. My dad who loved me and who'd never wanted anything but the very best for me.

He'd lain there, sobbing, a silent weeping as he'd tried to pull himself together pretending that everything was fine, small gasps of air into the Christmas night, all alone because I'd left him.

Andreas was here holding me. I could only hope Thomas was there to hold Dad now, bringing him back up from the darkness, once again, this time caused by me, the son who loved them both.

Everything just felt empty now, my soul, my mind, my body, but it was something that had played on my mind for so long, some kind of wicked need to finally tell my dad about it. I should have told him years ago. The grown-up me knew I should have talked to someone when I was still at school, my dads, one of them, perhaps even the school nurse, anyone who could have told me that I was both right and wrong and helped me manage my fears, helped me handle them when they became overwhelming, when they threatened to eat me alive when I saw my dad suffer and had me dreading picking up the phone when I got an unexpected call from Thomas or an unknown number.

I regretted telling Dad about it. I couldn't even imagine how he felt now on top of everything else. I was devastated, crushed, desperate, falling. He was probably feeling the same, only a hundred times worse. I was a grown-up and should have kept my mouth shut. Perhaps he hated me as much as I hated myself.

A soft knock on the door pulled me out of my spiralling thoughts. I could feel Andreas moving around me, feel him open his mouth as if to ward off whoever it was.

"Can I come in?" Thomas. Of course it was. Here to tell me off for my insanely insensitive behaviour.

Andreas nodded, his chin bumping uncomfortably against the top of my head like he was absolutely agreeing with me.

The mattress dipped as Thomas sat, and I once again felt like a naughty child. Andreas held me tighter as I closed my eyes and curled myself against his chest. He smelled so good—sweat, dinner, the smells from the cooking, coffee, wine, his cologne and something undefined that was only him, my Andreas.

Thomas just sat there, probably watching me. That was what he usually did when he didn't say anything. I imagined him biting his lip, shaking a bit as he wondered if he could touch me or not, folding his hands in his lap to keep them somewhere, but he would soon reach for me.

The rustling sound and the slight change in the mattress told me before I felt his hand on my shoulder. He cleared his throat, and I braced myself.

"What happened, Fredrik?" His voice was low, but there was no accusation in it. He drew his breath before continuing. "Frank was totally destroyed last night, wouldn't stop crying. The nurse is with him now, but... he...he wouldn't tell me what you'd said, just that he had failed and that you hated him."

"I don't hate him! I love him!" The thought of hating him was almost unbearable. I never had. Never would. My voice was back, and my eyes were wide open as Andreas placed a hand on my shoulder, trying to calm me down.

"I know, son." Thomas's hand hugged my arm. "I know. But what happened?"

"I told him that I was afraid he'd kill himself. I've always been terrified of him finally killing himself."

"Huh. Why?" Thomas seemed surprised and confused. "He's pretty stable now. His medicines are working, and mentally he hasn't had a really bad episode for several years."

"No, not now. When I was a kid. Since I was ten."

His movement stilled. "What?"

Andreas answered for me. "He read up on bipolarity when he was ten and found out about the suicide rates. Since then, he's been obsessively afraid that Frank would kill himself." His voice was clear and strong, to the point, the way Thomas liked it.

"Oh, Fredrik." Dad was suddenly leaning over me, his arms around my chest. He was actually crushing me, but his movement was so fast and unexpected that I didn't care. I just wanted to lie there, between these two men I loved, in an infinite loss of the third one.

"I'm so sorry," he muttered against my neck. "So, so sorry." His body shivered, like he was crying, and I wanted so badly to hug him. I wanted to be hugged. So I sank into my boyfriend's arms and let them both hug me, trying to be in the moment, feel their bodies comfort me, feel my own body, not think about Frank, not think about his pain, my pain, our pain, not now.

"I am so sorry," Thomas said again. "I...we thought it was the right thing to do. Telling you."

"It was," I spluttered in protest. "It was! I wanted to know. I needed to know! It was my own fault for not asking more, for googling, for not understanding what I was actually reading, and that I needed to talk to someone..." I was blabbering now, spilling words that I wasn't sure made any sense.

"No, it wasn't your fault." Both of them said it, Andreas' soft voice at the same time as the desperate voice of my dad.

"It wasn't, Fredrik." Dad was calmer now, which calmed me a little. "We should have seen it. Should have understood that you would try to find more information on your own. You were never the kind of kid who was happy with just being told that something was black and white. You always researched. Read up on things. Watched YouTube."

I smiled. I supposed I'd always been a researcher. I was never satisfied with normal books. I wanted references, fact-checking, thick books full of things I didn't know I could know, so turning to the internet was just a normal thing in my life. Of course I knew not everything on the internet was fact-checked, and I would normally turn to balanced sources, to peer-reviewed books in the library, and discuss it with someone. But this matter was too much, and after I'd read that article I just couldn't handle more. The words were already etched into my mind, and I didn't want to read them anymore.

"I need to see Dad," I muttered. I just had to feel him, to touch him, pull him towards me, know that he was still here and let him know I was too.

They let go of me, reluctantly, hands still holding on to me as I got up and stumbled across the room, leaving them both sat in my bed as I wandered off. It was early; I could tell from the darkness outside and the quietness of the house. There was just a small light from Dad's bedroom and the quiet movements of the night nurse.

I had to do this on my own. I had to apologise for telling him, for ruining this Christmas, this night, this moment. I needed to deliver some kind of apology, and deep down I needed to hear him say that he was sorry too, that they didn't see the burden they'd given me to carry. I was whining like a toddler, and I couldn't bear myself.

The nurse was just leaving as I walked into the room, and I nodded absentmindedly as I joined my dad in his bed. He was curled under the covers, facing the wall in the dim light. I could faintly see his hair on the pillow, only illuminated by the yellow glow from the lights outside seeping in between the curtains. He shivered beside me, as if he wanted to shrug away from whoever had entered his space. He always did. The nurse had showered him and sorted out his drips and meds, and it made him cold and exhausted.

I fluffed up the duvet, an endless piece of soft fabric enclosing us. It felt a mile long as I lifted it up and left it to slowly cover our bodies.

He was stiff against my arm. He tried to push me away, his strength almost frightening me, but I was stronger, and I put my arm around him and forced him towards me. He stilled for a few seconds, then fell into my arms, relaxing and becoming soft again.

He finally let me in. I could finally lie there, close to him, feel his heartbeat against my palm and his chest moving steadily, in and out. I could rest here, just like I'd wanted to when I was a kid, and this time he wouldn't be pushing me away. His temperature felt fine, something that further calmed my worries.

We'd both shed a lot of tears last night, and now I was once more the little ten-year-old boy, scared of the realities appearing around me. But this time, my dad was here, finally here, holding, consoling, assuring me that even though realities may be harsh, they would tell me about them when it became necessary, and I realised that the fear of my dad taking his own life was not the worst one, even if it was the most devastating one. What I feared most was that they wouldn't tell me, that they would shield me against the reality, that they would think it was in my interest not to know. But I already knew, so I had to know.

"My beautiful, wonderful son. Don't ever think I would do anything like that. Even in my worst state of mind, I would never have left you. You have to know that," he whispered in my ear as my tears fell again.

"I never understood…" I started, but I couldn't finish it. It wasn't important anymore. "I'm so scared of losing you," I said instead.

"You won't lose me," he lied. Because one day, I would, and things would never be the same again.

"I don't know how I'm supposed to deal with…with everything. I'm terrified, and yet I'm happy. I've got Andreas, and my life is supposed to be great, but I feel guilty even thinking that. He wants me to come with him back home, and how can I? I need to be here, and yet I can't *not* be where he is and…Dad? I don't know how I'm supposed to feel."

"None of us know how we're supposed to feel. This isn't something that comes with a textbook, and it's not something we can read a thesis on and figure out an answer. This is life, right here. Right now. You know that, right? There is no right and no wrong. Ever."

Trust Frank to know the right answer. I just held on to him as he continued to speak.

"One day, things will just change, and I may no longer be here. But that doesn't mean more than that. You will still be the brilliant man that you are, and you will have your Andreas, and the two of you will go on to live the most wonderful life. I know that. I can see it. And you will be happy because that is just the way things will be. You have always been happy when he was with you."

I snivelled and wiped my tears on the duvet.

"Things will always change, but that is just the way things are, and there is nothing we can do to stop it. But the one thing I can promise you is this. Listen, and listen well. I would never have left you. And if I one day in the future do, then it's not my choice. You hear me? It will never be my choice because if I could choose anything right now, I would choose to live. Here. I would choose to stay in this damn house with Thomas and just sit on that sofa out there and read the news and drink coffee and travel and go on a cruise. Thomas always talked about going on a cruise. We never did, and now I want to. Fuck life, eh?"

He laughed softly, and I did too.

"So instead, you are going to promise me this, son. You're going to go out there and live. From this day on, you're going to be fearless. Do all those things you want to. Travel. Learn. Read. Eat all the stupid foods we see on TV. Learn to cook. Meet people."

"I cook fine," I protested. He just laughed.

"You do. And you're a good baker too. Maybe not much of an artist, but you're a fine knitter. Make me another jumper. The last one you made is far too big for me now."

"I haven't knitted in years."

"Then start again. But while we're here, can you promise me one more thing?" He coughed, a dry painful cough that made me sit up and pull him towards me. I shoved the damn pillows up against his back and adjusted the drip attached to his arm.

"Yes," I said, surprised that my voice was as steady as it was. He laughed and reached up to wipe a tear from my eye.

"Things will be fine. They always are. And you will be fine. We all will be. Promise me you will remember that. Even when things are dark, you will be fine. Hold on to that boy of yours, and whenever you feel like things are about to crumble?"

"Yeah?"

He smiled and lay back against the pillows again.

"Bake a fucking loaf of bread. Makes everything better."

I laughed again, and so did he—an almost hysterical laugh where my chest hurt and Frank coughed, which only made us laugh more.

***

When I woke up later on Christmas Day, it was with my dad's arm on one side of me and Andreas sitting on the edge of the bed with a cup of coffee in his hand. Thomas stood in the doorway, and there was the familiar sound of Christmas coming from the living room.

"Lazy," Thomas said. "Most of us have already been out for a walk, and here you are, having a lie-in like there's nothing at all to do in the world."

"You're apparently on washing up duty," Andreas said with a grin, taking a sip from his cup. "And I'm on Frank duty because that drip is empty and it hurts my nursing soul." He put the cup down and reached for the gloves on the bedside table, before pushing my legs out of the way so he could get comfortable next to Frank.

"Oh, gosh, it's that German nurse again. Where on earth did you find this one?" Frank muttered.

"Oh, Mr Strand. We're not being rude to the nursing staff again, are we? I promise, I will be very gentle." Andreas put on an even stronger accent than he already had, and Frank huffed out a little laugh, stretching his arms up in the air.

"See? I think you should get up, Mr Strand. None of this lazing about in bed. I think some TV and cake is in order, and perhaps— Now I am going to moan at the nursing staff. Who the hell did this cannula? Looks like a right car-crash job. Sorry, Frank, this might hurt for a second, just let me... There you go."

"Monsters. All of you." Frank groaned.

"Absolutely. Now, this is my favourite part. I may be a very nice nurse, but I'm going to show you how to do a perfect job. Pay attention to my superior skills, Freddie. Pass me that tray over there?"

"Idiot." I laughed and did as I was told.

"I'm leaving." Thomas turned around and walked out the door. He'd always been squeamish, and I wasn't much better. Not like Andreas and his passion for needles and weird obsession with my dad's medical equipment.

My body was screaming for more sleep, and for a brief moment, I considered going back to my own bed to grab a few more hours, but I only made it as far as the kitchen before being sat down by a dishevelled Maria while she made me coffee. A triple espresso topped with water, just what my mind needed.

"You absolute dickwad," she hissed in disgust.

Then we sat there without saying anything because what could I respond to that?

"I can't talk, though, the number of times I have told the dads they've ruined my life. It's true because...you know. Impossible standards? God help anyone I decide to have a relationship with."

"But you have that...what's his name?"

"Matias. Broke up with him months ago. Didn't want to tell Frank. He really liked him, and...well. Turned out I didn't."

I smiled and reached for her hand. She pulled it away.

"Should we do something? Think about lunch? Make a quick round of bread?" She deflected, picking at the crumbs gathered in a neat pile on the tablecloth. She'd been here a while then, listening in, trying to rescue the clearly tense mood in the house.

"Nah. Let's just have coffee and relax," I said. The brown elixir was slowly seeping into my brain, making me feel more normal again. If people wanted to eat, they could come eat.

"Thank you for my presents. I loved the clothes," I said quietly.

"Someone has to dress you. That Cali vibe you have going on here won't cut it in Germany."

"Who said I'm going to Germany?"

"Dude." She smiled. I smiled back. Yeah.

"I love you." Her voice was strong, and she finally let me take her hand. "Don't be a dick. Not this time. Enough dicking around."

"I like dicking around," I smarmed back as she rolled her eyes.

"You do indeed. I mean, you never came out or anything. I thought you were straight. All my life, and then suddenly you were snogging 'Dreas, and everyone was okay with it? Had that been me—"

"I would have killed you. Honestly." I laughed. "'Dreas is mine. No sharing."

"Oh, fuck you, Fredrik." She was laughing, and I took the last sip from my coffee.

"I didn't even know myself. It's not like everyone has these big revelations as toddlers and knows exactly who they are. I never did. I didn't know. It was just...you know? A connection. I never understood it, but I've only ever had it with him. Him and me. We just, you know, fit?"

"Told you. Impossible standards to live up to. I'll never fit. I just don't. I'm a square peg in a round hole. Men are scared of me, and women? I'm not sure. I'm intimidating according to my last assessment chat with our head of education. Five-star rating in the classroom but must try harder not to frighten my colleagues."

"Sounds about right."

"Sounds crazy."

"Maria, you're awesome. And perhaps that's all you need to be?"

"Nah. I need that tin of toffees over there and a good film on TV. Wanna join me before I go all sappy and cry my eyes out?"

"Sounds like a plan."

Everything was like it was yesterday—the Christmas tree, the decorations, the big dinner table with the white tablecloth against the bright red amaryllis bulbs—but not the mess of dirty plates, crumbs and napkins left on the coffee table. Breakfast had obviously been had out here, glasses sparkling despite their greasy spots. The pile of gifts was long gone, of course. Two bags filled to the brim with used paper were waiting next to the tree instead, ready to be taken to the recycling centre.

I took a seat next to my sister, but before I could get too comfortable, Lilly rolled in and, typically, arranged herself on my lap.

"Freddie," she whined.

"Hungover much, Lils?"

"Yeah. I blame Maria." She glared at my sister before dumping her head back down on my lap with a thud.

I stroked her hair, all tangled strands and streaks of bleached shades. The freckles on her cheeks stood proud against her pale skin. She was always more beautiful in winter, when her tan faded and she took on that ethereal waif look. All colours and sparkles, and like today, a slight sour whiff of alcohol still lingering on her breath.

"Lils, are you okay?" I asked carefully, as she retched and violently shook her head.

"Nah. But nothing a good breakfast won't cure. I'm never drinking again."

"And I'm never playing poker with you guys again. What was that? I mean?" Maria was laughing, so I took that as a good sign.

"Don't blame me. Papi won, and Vati is still salty about it. You're crap at poker, Maria. No poker face. You and I need to sit down and work on that. Deal?"

"Deal. But I don't think I can drink again tonight. I think Dry January is well in order next year. No more drinking. A healthy lifestyle. Back to the gym..."

"And all that shit that none of us will stick to. Not even Vati."

"Did I hear my name mentioned?" And there was Gabriel, swanning around in his new robe, a bright-red one with the labels still attached, proudly stroking the fabric as he took a seat next to Maria. "What are we watching?"

"Trying to find something good."

"Needs to be cheesy," Gabriel insisted, grabbing a toffee from Maria's tin.

"Absolutely," I agreed. "The more cheese the better."

"Gorgonzola," Lilly added.

"Parmigiano," Andreas shouted from the bedroom.

"Mozzarella!" Frank added in a high-pitched voice.

"Wait for me!" And there was Thomas, grabbing his chair before Bruno entered the room with a sigh and disappeared again.

"Movie morning!" Maria shouted. "I'm pressing play. Get here or miss the start."

"Hold your horses," Bruno called from the kitchen. "What are we watching?"

I didn't really care. As long as I had my family, perhaps Frank was right. For now, everything was fine.

"Who ate the last of the brown cheese?" Lottie appeared, looking flustered with a packet of butter in one hand and a piece of bread in the other.

"Oh. There's no more brown cheese? But is there any food? Have you baked?" Lilly was already on her way into the kitchen again before stopping and retching in the doorway. She disappeared, and we didn't bother yelling after her.

For once, we let the awkwardness remain, leaving it for another time. We were good at talking in this family, sometimes too good, but sometimes we were good at leaving it, too, and of course sometimes even too good at that. I knew Frank and I needed to talk about his illness again, when we were less emotional, less stressed, less tired. I needed to understand, put things into perspective. Until then, we would cope, we always did, and we did that by living, drinking coffee, having dinner, snowball fights and movie nights in the middle of the day, friendly fighting, hugging and bantering, and some late-night wine that may have touched on new issues without really touching them.

Chapter Sixteen
Gabriel

When I was a small child, before...well, I always referred to it as *the before*, I dreamed of having this big, blended rainbow family. I used to borrow books from the library, big clunky textbooks on the process of adoption. I used to pray that I would find a boy who would love me, the real me, sweeping in like a gallant knight riding a purple glittery unicorn, and then we would just find these stray children and make ourselves a family. Little did I know that only a few years later I would fracture the only family I'd ever had. I left them behind, ran away and never came back. I wasn't welcome anyway. It took my older sister a few weeks to find me, and when she did, I told her to forget that I'd ever existed. I hadn't seen her since.

I sometimes retold Bruno the whole story when he was at his lowest. Then I'd tell him that I loved him and that true love lasted a lifetime. I'd tell him that I loved our kids, so much that my chest would sometimes feel like it was about to explode. I loved them even when I shouted at them and screamed and threatened them with various things that I never managed to fully implement. I'd shut off the Wi-Fi. They'd hack the router. I'd tell them that I'd stop paying their phone contracts. To be honest, I had no idea where I would go to cancel them. I made empty threats that I'd always fail to carry through. I loved my family too much to care.

I sometimes shuddered at how easily my life could have taken a different path. I could have been the kid on the streets, the nameless victim in the news. I could have lost out on all this, and it still made me want to cry.

It was my parents who'd lost out, and they'd not only lost out on their youngest child, the one that was defective. That was what my father had called it, having a defect. I was supposed to conform to their ideals and traditions and make them proud. If that had been me? My kids? What were they thinking? Did they have so little love for me that they just let me go? I would have fought for my three, fought every battle on the frontline with my shield and sword. I would have died for my family, and that was no lie.

Which brought me back to the man who slept peacefully in the bed next to me. It was New Year's Day, and just like that, another year had gone by. Yesterday had been a good day. Frank had been up for most of it, and we'd done all the usual things last night. Fancy dinner, folded napkins and bottle after bottle of wine. We'd watched silly things on TV, played that ancient board game that Thomas rolled out every year, and then we'd drunk some more. Had dessert. Toasted in champagne and watched the sky explode outside, colours lighting up the world.

A whole year gone, a year that hadn't stood out too much from the one before. The girls were well on their way to finding careers. Andreas was amazing. He was so passionate about his work, about his kids, his people, and now he had his Freddie back, a reality that filled me both with calm and a tiny bit of dread.

I smiled to myself and scratched the greying hair on my head. Bruno's had gone all thin and straggly, while mine was still as thick as always. I was his silver fox, he would tease. He was, in return, my nutty professor, the man who still made me laugh every day. He was so bloody stupid and pig-headed at times. Other times, he overwhelmed me with emotions. Sometimes he made me so angry that all I could do was scream. But he was mine. Always.

Andreas, though, I'd lost my shit with him the other day, and I'd finally managed to apologise last night. Which was good. I hoped. He wasn't a child anymore. He was a man, making his own path in life, and despite all my reservations, he belonged with the tall, blond man who made his face light up like a beacon. Those two boys were meant to be from the very first moment they'd met. Fredrik, tall, clever, so bright. Fredrik, who carried so much of his father's load, seeming so much older than his years, then suddenly he would somehow become a silly child, playing the fool and making us laugh, and the next minute you would find him coming into the kitchen just to wrap his arms around Andreas's waist, and he would just stand there, breathing in the calm that he somehow seemed to find in my chaotic son.

Andreas had struggled, but he was a different man today. He smiled more. He had plans, and he had excitedly hugged me and told me to prepare for chaos, as he was bringing his Freddie home. We didn't mind; of course we didn't. It was no secret there had been tension in this house over the last couple of days, but we were not those kind of friends. Not that kind of people. We had always lived with mood swings and exhaustion and sadness and grief. We'd also lived with love and hugs and laughter. We'd made a pact of respect many years ago, Frank and me. We'd sat in a park somewhere and he'd taken my hand and promised me we'd never fall out or cause drama that wasn't there. We'd had to learn to share small spaces and go for walks when things became too much. We'd also figured out how to read his moods, and he, in return, read us back.

I couldn't quite remember what had triggered that bench-sitting moment anyway, some imbecilic disagreement over bags in the hallway or dirty shoes worn in the house. It hadn't mattered anyway because here we were, ten years later, the only family we all had, and still we threw ourselves into the fire and spent all our holidays together. Because we always had. Even though Frank had been all tears the other day and Fredrik had skulked around like the world was hanging around his shoulders...well, I hadn't got the full story out of Frank, he wasn't ready to talk to me yet, and Fredrik had predictably closed in on himself. He was okay, Andreas had assured me. Just figuring things out.

I'd always wanted a big, messy, chaotic rainbow family. I wanted unconditional love. I wanted my children to be close, tied by invisible bonds of support and belonging. Bonds that I would never allow them to break.

I left Bruno in the bed where we'd slept every Christmas for the last ten years. It was home, like the cottage at Aunt Bella's, like our flat in the leafy part of Berlin. I closed the door gently and wrapped the dressing gown around my body. My body. It was mine, and I'd grown into it like a comfortable old pair of slippers. It wasn't perfect and never would be, but it was what I'd been dealt, and however much I'd tried to change it, it had always fought back. Now it was what it was. Mine. Firm and muscular and jaded in places, but it also bore the scars of a life of struggles and the birth of my brood.

I gave birth to three babies, who had grown into beautiful souls. Well, they swore like those gangsters on TV, had zero table manners and completely failed at ever cleaning the bathroom, but they had other traits that I admired, and these bloody kids made me so fucking proud. Pardon the language.

Andreas. The one who'd gifted me all my grey hairs.

Lilly, so strong and proud. The bearer of traditions and organiser of outings. She had the kindest heart. I was so proud of her.

Lottie had a way with Frank, where she wrapped him around her fingers and made him smile with no expectations in return. She indulged him and praised him, and he proudly showed me the texts she'd sent him. He loved her like a daughter. I had no idea where life would take her, but I hoped it would be one hell of a ride.

Maria. Proud, stubborn Maria.

Fredrik. He'd always have a special place in my old, jaded heart.

"Love is not defined by blood," Frank had said to me one evening on some beach in Portugal, another holiday among all those we had spent together. "Maria and Fredrik carry none of my genes, none of my blood. Does that mean I love them any less than Thomas does, who is their biological father? Nope. It has never meant shit. Those kids were mine from the first time I saw them, and I don't care what science or any kind of paperwork tries to prove. I am their father. They are my kids. Same goes for yours. If anything ever happened to me or Thomas—"

"Nothing is ever going to happen to you or Thomas," I'd interrupted. Because that's what you said, despite knowing how fragile life could be.

"If anything happened to you or Bruno, do you think we would abandon the kids? I would be on the next plane to bring them home, you need to know that. They would be looked after, however we had to change our lives to fit. Lils and Lotts and Andreas are my kids too," he'd said in a stern voice that I knew better than to argue with.

"Our kids love each other," I'd replied. "They are family, and I hope they will always be."

"Some of our kids love each other a little more than the others." He'd laughed.

Yeah, like we didn't all know. Andreas and Fredrik had been laying in the sand, further away, their hands entwined and their feet touching, talking animatedly to each other like teenage boys did. They had always been something else and still were. As my son came stumbling into the kitchen, his chest bare and wearing Fredrik's joggers, even I knew that.

"Morning," he said and snuggled into my embrace. He was still sleep warm, smelling of sheets and sweat and...yeah. My son had sex. It was still something I cringed over having to process.

"Hi, my baby," I whispered.

He plonked himself down at the table, like the spoilt brat he was, while I moved around the kitchen like it was my own, opening the cupboards and putting my hands on the things I needed without looking. I'd always felt at home here, with the familiar-looking packets and chipped coffee cups and mismatched plates. We didn't even bring our own coffee anymore, Thomas having Bruno's favourite blend delivered here twice a year. He drank it himself, saying the flavour reminded him of good times.

I pressed the button on the coffee maker, and sat down opposite my son, reaching out to grab his hands. I stroked them, young, soft skin against my gravelly, dry fingers.

"How are you?" I asked quietly. "Are you coping with all this?"

"I'm good," he said, his smile reassuring. "I just feel...Vati, I feel like such a fool. I've wasted all this time being stupid and pigheaded. I should have spent the last couple of years in America with Freddie. I should have been there with him, supporting him. I should have been happy, instead of dragging my feet in Berlin, letting the best years of my life waste away."

"Life moves in mysterious ways," I said, laughing at myself trying to be all old and wise. I was neither. "But had you gone with him to America, perhaps you wouldn't have made it. Perhaps it would have broken both of you. Instead, you grew up and both of you figured out what you really wanted."

"I want him. I need to be with him because he makes me a better person. I am calmer with him. Things are less chaotic in my head when he's next to me. It sounds weird, but he's always calmed me down. I never had to be anything because he didn't want me to be anything else but myself. I fucked that up, so badly. I hurt him, Vati, and now I feel like I have to spend the rest of my life making it up to him."

"I spent years thinking I had ruined your Papi's life—everyone's life, darling. Don't ride that guilt trip. You have to let it all go, all that happened in the past, and let it be that. Something that just simply happened. There's nothing you can do to change it, so you need to focus all your energy now on being happy. If you're happy, Fredrik will be happy. I don't have to tell you all this because you already know it. But that's not what I meant. Are you okay? Are you coping? You know, it's no good for any of us to hold things in."

"This? This has been hard, I admit that. But Freddie is talking. I'm talking. We're just slowly letting things become something we can work with, and I think that's all we have to be now. A work in progress. He needs to get things out, process, and I think he's doing that. And. Well. I'm glad I'm here, Vati. I hate to think what would have happened if I hadn't been. I needed to be here for Freddie. Frank—he's strong, so unbelievably strong."

"Frank has been my best friend for years. I don't know what I would have done without him."

"You would have spent more time with your children and not been so obsessed with social media."

"I was his PA for a while when he was half famous. Of course I had to be obsessed with social media."

"You can be my PA, give up teaching and just make me into one of those influencers, and I'll make loads of dosh just sitting around on beaches. Why haven't you done that? What kind of dad are you?"

"And then you'd be all famous and more messed up in the head than you already are? You'd never make it as a celeb."

"I'd be a brilliant celeb," he argued. I loved seeing him smile. "But no. No thanks. I'll stay here, quietly in the background."

"Just don't be a dick," Bruno said, stumbling into the room, ruffling his son's hair and then smacking his palm on our firstborn's shoulder. Then he just stood there, stunned, like he had completely forgotten what he was going to do.

"I won't be a dick." Andreas pouted at him for bringing that one up again. "No more dicking around. One day I will figure out how to be all sensible and nice and grown up, doing grown-up shit, not fucking up. You know. Normal stuff."

Our son was a dick. There was no point beating around that bush.

"You just need to not go on holiday with the love of your life, and you need not to invite some girl who has an obvious infatuation with you, to stay with you, and then you need not to pretend that you're interested in her, and perhaps you should not make her sleep in your room. That one was on us. We should have put our foot down and said no," Bruno said, with a pained voice.

"I was a stupid kid, Papi." Andreas sighed. "You never said no to anything I did. And even if you had said no, I would have brought her anyway. I was being a dick, remember?"

"You were a complete twatface," Bruno agreed like it was normal and okay. It was neither.

"Bruno, let's not drag up the past." I tried to keep my voice soft because there was nothing more unattractive than a full-blown family argument early in the morning when staying with friends. Good start to a new year too. Andreas moaned, sensing my total discomfort with where this conversation was heading.

"The kid needs to hear it." Bruno grunted and pulled out a chair and sat himself down, grabbing and sipping my coffee with a satisfied hum.

"I only did it because I was angry at him," Andreas muttered. "And I was a freaking child. I mean, it was years ago."

"You had a girl sleeping in your room—a girl who was totally besotted with you—and where did you sleep at night, kid?" The way Bruno stared at Andreas he could've just admitted to running off with some terror group. Well, same. Same, same.

"I slept on the floor next to his bed. He wouldn't let me lie next to him," my son admitted, and he couldn't even look up.

"*That* was the problem," Bruno said, like he was surgically removing that small blot of a disaster from our collective memories. Talk about a week full of tension, despite all nine of us staying in a house the size of a small castle—with one infatuated young German Cinderella in tow.

"I know," Andreas admitted, and for once he was sitting up, his back straight and he was actually looking straight at his father. Wow. "I was in love with him and at the same time I hated him. I couldn't sleep if he wasn't next to me, yet he didn't want me there, and I wanted to be anywhere but where he was. I wanted to run away and never come back. But I needed to be with him, like, all the time. It was a lot for my fried brain to understand. I didn't know how to fix it apart from...yeah. I fucked up."

"You were with him, all right. We all heard that part. And I drove the poor girl to the station the next day." Bruno slammed his cup down on the table and stared at our son. "And I'm not bringing all this up because I'm a dick. Well, maybe I am a bit of a dick too at times, but I'm telling you so you remember what you did. Because I think before you decide on any kind of future, you should probably go out there and find Fredrik and apologise the shit out of yourself for that little spectacle. Nothing is going to move forward until you do. Say sorry. End of."

"Enough!" I said. I knew where this discussion would go. We'd had it before, but for the first time, Andreas seemed to understand. Like we were finally on the same page.

"I know." Andreas sounded deflated again. "And I have apologised. To you too. Sorry. That was unreasonable and twattish behaviour from a much younger me who promises I'll not be a dick in the future. And can we please make a pact not to bring this up ever again? Turn a new leaf and all that?"

"What are we supposed to do? Erase it from our memories?" Lottie swept past, her hair tousled and messy, wearing some ridiculous penguin onesie as she elbowed her way onto Bruno's lap, blowing me a kiss in the process.

"Not even a proper Happy New Year's kiss?" I waved my fist in the air, and she just laughed, my beautiful girl.

"Don't be a dick," Bruno said sternly, staring down our son across the table. "That single summer changed your whole life. And Freddie's. That's what you need to remember and learn from. I didn't see it then, and I'm sorry I didn't do better. Somewhere we, as your parents, should have interfered. But then again..."

"I won't be a dick," Andreas said back, his gaze firm on my husband.

"I agree," Lottie snorted. "Don't fuck up. Maria will have your balls on a plate if you do, and I will be right there helping her remove them."

"I'm a surgeon. I could remove your balls in your sleep and you wouldn't even know what had hit you," my darling husband muttered.

"Bruno!" I boomed. Now we were taking this a little too far.

"Good one, Papi." Lottie laughed and fist-bumped her Papi, who was just laughing like he was some stupid teenager. Well, he still was, damn it.

"Behave," I said and sighed because kids. People. I kind of just wanted to go back to bed and read my book and be left to chill for a while.

"Morning!" Thomas called far too cheerfully, waltzing through the door and picking up a cup from the dish rack on the way. He stopped and stared at us. "Where's the champagne?"

"Oh shit. I left it out in the snow last night, it will be frozen solid by now!" Bruno scrambled up, almost dropping Lottie on the floor as he moved towards the front door and bumped into Fredrik, carrying an armful of champagne bottles.

"I rescued them," he said triumphantly, winking at Bruno, who relieved him of his load and lined the bottles up on the worktop as Lottie started lifting down glasses from the draining rack.

"Where're Lils and Maria?" Fredrik asked, walking over and giving Andreas a quick kiss. Oh, my boy.

I was going all soppy in my old age. Andreas looked so happy that it broke my heart to realise how unhappy he must have been without this guy. Fredrik. The guy who was now thundering up the stairs causing havoc, as we could hear the girls screaming upstairs, no doubt from him throwing himself on their beds, pulling off blankets, squirting them with water. All the normal stuff.

We were back to normality, everyone talking in a mishmash of languages, doors slamming, coffee being poured and champagne corks being fired at the ceiling, the dents joining the previous ten years' worth, marking their place in the history of this family. We had the same on our kitchen ceiling in Berlin. Cork marks and memories filled with laughter.

Frank appeared, dragging his drip stand along with his fist in the air, complaining that the cripple needed his beauty sleep and what was all this racket about? He demanded his drip be filled with champagne and suddenly we were all cramped into this small suburban kitchen, holding up glasses and toasting to the first day of the new year like we'd always done every New Year's Day morning. We toasted to friendships. To new beginnings. To not being a dick, and to liking dicks too because it seemed we all did. To Andreas and Fredrik for *finally* getting their *shit together*. That one was all on Lilly, while I was threatening to wash my darling daughter's mouth out with soap.

Finally, we toasted to love, in all shapes and forms, in whatever way it would find us. We toasted to being loved. To family. To us. Because without each other, to quote my daughter again, where the fuck would we have been and what the hell would we have become?

Chapter Seventeen
Maria

THE HOUSE WAS empty. Quiet. Deafeningly silent, in fact, and after almost two weeks of constant noise, the lack of it hurt my head.

It had been two comfortable weeks. Cosy, overwhelming, full of people with not a second alone except in the bathroom, and for some of us not even that had been a solo moment, but comfortable.

Just as suddenly as they had arrived, they were gone. All of them. Thomas and Fredrik had gone with everyone to the airport, Fredrik having packed his stuff only a week after unpacking it since he'd decided he was going with Andreas, and who knew when he'd be back here again. He said two weeks so he could spend more time with Frank and also get the rest of his things. I'd booked him the ticket and Frank had just laughed. He'd be back, but I had a feeling things had changed for the better for my brother. There was a calmness in him that calmed me too.

The whirlwinds known as Lilly and Lottie were no longer occupying my bed and leaving my room in a mess. I really didn't know why Dad was so insistent that I cleaned and tidied here before they'd arrived. Once their suitcases were opened, the room had looked like an explosion anyway with clothes strewn all over the floor, hung on any hook and covering my chairs. We'd all slept in my king-size bed, which left more floor space, not that there was much of that anyway. Maybe it was weird the three of us still sleeping here together, but traditions were traditions, and it strangely made sense.

My little sisters were just that, and I'd loved every messy moment of having them near.

I looked around and sighed. I should clean up, pack my bag, throw the linen and the pile of towels lying in a corner in the washing machine, vacuum, empty the rubbish, take the empty champagne bottles to the recycling, or at least put them in a bag by the door so Dad could take them later. After all, it was their house. They'd fix it. But I could still pretend to be grown up and responsible, something I didn't feel like right now. I didn't want to tidy them away; I wished they were still here, and once I'd cleaned up, Christmas would be over. I wasn't ready for that. Not yet.

I groaned and sat on the edge of the bed, closed my eyes and rested my elbows on my knees. The weight on the small, hard spots was uncomfortable, but I didn't have energy to move my arms into a better position. My eyes were sore, and my body exhausted. I'd never realised how much invisible energy it took to try to keep everything together and pretend everything was normal when every damn breath hurt. Even when I'd concentrated on my breathing, slow light ones in through my nose, deep blows out of my mouth, my chest still reeled with a pain I couldn't shift. I didn't want to cry now. I wasn't lonely. I was just tired after two weeks of intense family life. Two weeks of trying not to fall apart. I'd scolded my brother for not holding it together as well as I had, and now I felt even worse because I had.

I didn't know if I'd ever have my own family, not besides the one I got at birth, I mean, and Lotts and Lils and the others, but that was not what I meant now. Dating had bruised me—my heart and my ego and my stupid, stupid self—and I was slowly coming to terms with likelihood that I'd one day be an old spinster with nothing to show for my life. My last relationship still stabbed me in the heart, just thinking about it. Another pathetic mistake. Another man who I'd thought would make a difference. Someone to fall in love with.

I thought I had, again. I thought I had found the one, the one to share my life with, the one I wanted, but I'd started doubting more the longer I stayed with him.

Not doubting men in general because I was definitely into men like the rest of my family, or "Bei uns geht ohne Schwanz nix!" as Lottie would shout at the top of her voice when drunk. I liked dick too. At least, most of the time. I'd once met this Belgian beauty at a party in Antwerp when

I visited a friend there. She was genuinely beautiful, very sexy and had the moves of another world, but she was not the one either. Just a fling.

Apparently, my ex had also been a fling. Matias, short and dark and virile, his parents from Argentina, had been dancing tango since he was five. We'd connected over values and causes, all those things we wanted to achieve, and we'd seemed to align well. He wanted to go to Latin America to work, plant trees, save the jungle, small monkeys, snakes and medical plants. His plans were as grandiose as he was inspiring and eager.

I wanted to go with him, not because it was *him*, of course, but because the causes were important, something to live for, something to sacrifice my current life for. I could teach there, Science, Maths, English, discover gifted kids and help them into the future. I started learning Spanish because Matias and his plans had me fooled for a while.

We'd talked about travelling to Argentina, Ecuador, Guatemala. Teaching and planting, cleaning seabirds and marking penguin nests, doing what a lot of wealthy kids do, according to others. I'd travelled before, gone on epic adventures, and it had suddenly all felt too much. Too childish.

As his engagement grew, mine shrank. His plans became less grandiose and appealing and more practical, drafting articles and making petitions and contacting people, and I was simply postponing it all, thinking I had no more energy to try to save the world anymore. All I had done was promise to fly less and eat more vegan food.

I'd finally got a permanent position as a teacher this year, something that was always really hard to get in Oslo, even if it was only in one of the mediocre suburban schools, not in any of the prestigious city schools or science-oriented colleges that I'd once aimed for, but it had been a good start to my career, and I wasn't ready to give it up. The job had made it possible for me to buy my own flat, not big or anything Instagram-worthy, just a one-bedroom, north-facing ground-floor apartment half an hour by metro then fifteen minutes' walk from the station, but it was mine and even sharing it with someone made me feel weirdly nauseous.

I'd called him on New Year's Eve. He'd been invited to celebrate with us, to have dinner here before the six of us went out, Lils and Lotts and the boys and us, but he'd bailed at the last second, claiming he took the tram in the wrong direction and now it would be too late. All the while he was talking, I could hear music and cheering in the background.

I didn't even suggest he could take an Uber. I just disconnected and went to dinner, muttering that he wasn't coming, and my family had kindly left it at that.

Maybe Matias was the one, even though it didn't feel like it. He was a nice guy, attractive and pleasant. The sex had been good. Or had it? I was constantly questioning myself these days. Not everyone could have the same relationship as Fredrik and Andreas or stay together for what would eventually be a lifetime, like my fathers or Gabriel and Bruno. And sometimes that lifetime would be cut short. I shrugged and pushed those thoughts away. Maybe I should have just settled with Matias, gone with the flow, travelled to the ends of the Earth to save the climate. I shouldn't have been so selfish and only thought about my job. Maybe my passions would one day come back—for Matias, the climate, the planet and politics and saving everything. Maybe I'd one day discover that he hadn't been the one after all. I wanted to scream at all the confusion in my head.

I sighed as I looked out of the window, the dark sky painting a dramatic backdrop to the naked apple trees, branches now covered in snow. The garden was peaceful, the snow muffling all the sounds, bushes looking like cotton buds with the trees weeping water from above.

It was so different from the view from my own flat. My glass-screened veranda was next to the parking lot, and even if the glass shielded some things I did get my fair share of vehicles and shouting from angry people when someone had taken their parking place. The snow there was never white, except if I peeked outside before anyone had moved their cars after a snowy night. The car park seemed to almost instantly transform into a grey, salty mass of sleet once the first couple of cars had moved.

My phone dinging from somewhere pushed my thoughts out of my pathetic self-reflection. I frantically tried to find it, as I couldn't remember where I'd put it.

It was stuck inside my pillow case. I didn't know how it had ended up there, of course. I thought I'd had it this morning, and then it shouldn't have been put back under my pillow, where I used to keep it at night, when there was at least one L between me and the bedside table.

I glanced at the screen. I had a few notifications from WhatsApp, Messenger and Tinder, which I had only because L&L had reinstalled it and turned on those dreaded notifs again, knowing full well I'd swipe left on all of them. They had tried to cheer me up and make me live again when

I'd just wanted to curl under the duvet and pretend life outside these walls didn't exist.

I ignored the Tinder ones and would uninstall that darned app later. The group chat with the family was alive and well, though.

GABRIEL: Fuck, we have to pay for five kilos overweight baggage.

BRUNO: What the heck? We were five kilos BELOW on the way here, and that was with the Christmas gifts.

THOMAS: FRANK...

FRANK: Umm. Might have added some apple juice. And apple jam. And apple butter. I wrapped them carefully so they wouldn't break.

LILLY: APPLE BUTTER (heart eye emoji)

LOTTIE: Apple juice (heart)

GABRIEL: My money... (dollar)

FRANK: Sorry. Just tell me how much so I can pay for it. Didn't mean to overload you, but you had tons of space.

BRUNO: That's because I brought five kilos of cheese and six bottles of Riesling for you. Bulky as shit. But don't worry. We'll pay. And enjoy the exclusive apple juice when we get home. No juice for Monday breakfast, Lottie. Only weekends!

LOTTIE: Tuesdays then?

BRUNO: Weekend!

LOTTIE: (heart eye)?

BRUNO: No, Lottie. WEEKENDS.

LILLY: Has anyone seen my purse?

LOTTIE: Have you checked your handbag? And pockets?

LILLY: YES!

LOTTIE: Inside your suitcase too? Don't you remember when Vati forgot the keys to our flat and had to pay a locksmith a fortune to get us in? And then he found them immediately once he started unpacking the suitcase.

GABRIEL: Enough!

LILLY: No, it's not there. @Maria, can you see if it's in your room?

LOTTIE: Or in the bathroom. Or in the kitchen. Or hallway. Or Fredrik's room.

LILLY: Ewwww, not Fredrik's room. It reeks.

LOTTIE: Of sex.

ANDREAS: Girls...

LOTTIE: Hey Dreas. Woken up from the sex haze yet? He-he.

LILLY: Sex arse?

LOTTIE: It rhymes! Sex haze, sex arse!

FREDRIK: More like sex ace.

ANDREAS: (heart) (aubergine) (ace)

LILLY: @Maria! Are you there?

MARIA: Sorry, couldn't find my phone. Can't find your purse either, Lilly. I've checked everywhere.

LOTTIE: Under the pillow too?

MARIA: Oh, there it is.

LOTTIE: I swear, that pillow swallows everything.

MARIA: Yeah, took my phone, too. Swallow pillow, it's almost a rhyme.

LILLY: But you found my purse? You are an angel (heart)

MARIA: Yeah, but how do I get it to you? Oh, I know, you can borrow money from Fredrik.

FREDRIK: From me?

MARIA: You're Lilly's family now, for real. You need to up your game to make sure they like you and accept you.

LOTTIE: Fuck, I've forgotten my pills.

MARIA: The antibabypills?

MARIA: God, I love that word. Antibabypille. Why isn't it called that in English?

LILLY: Because English is a shit language.

LOTTIE: Yes!

MARIA: Fuck.

LOTTIE: That was the plan...

LILLY: Maybe you can borrow them from Fredrik too, ha-ha. He is family!

GABRIEL: Is there anything you haven't told us, Fredrik?

LOTTIE: He's busy. Smooching Andreas.

FREDRIK: You can have my condoms.

LILLY: Don't you need them yourself?

ANDREAS: Ouch. Fredrik...

BRUNO: Don't you use condoms? Have you been tested? Both of you? You know that viruses can be dormant for a long time and you've only been back together for two weeks??

THOMAS: Fredrik, what's going on? We did have The Talk™ with you, didn't we?

FRANK: Yes, we did. Oh my god, we did.

THOMAS: Umm, yes we did.

FREDRIK: We're grown-ups, and besides, I trust him.

THOMAS: You can't trust anyone!

BRUNO: You can't trust anyone!

FREDRIK: Jeeeezuz.

LILLY: I think they left.

ANDREAS: Yes, we left you, idiots, and besides, it's only been Fredrik since forever. Well, if you count an aborted threesome.

FREDRIK: Andreas, maybe we should go to Copenhagen instead. Get a flat there and just ignore these people.

ANDREAS: Or Belgium. Antwerp, you could have that guest researcher's job you showed me?

FREDRIK: Or Rome. Or Madrid. Or Austin.

GABRIEL: Why Austin? Why not back to LA if you have to go to America?

FREDRIK: Well, Santa Barbara then. I can probably get a job at UCSB. At least teaching assistant. Get as far away from these horrible people as possible.

LOTTIE: Maria, can you see if you can find my pills?

MARIA: Any idea where?

LOTTIE: ...bathroom?

MARIA: Nope.

LILLY: The Swallow Pillow?

MARIA: Actually, there's a pack there. How come the Swallow Pillow swallows everything?

LOTTIE: Yay! But how do I get them back?

LILLY: Borrow condoms from Fredrik and get Maria to send you your pills.

MARIA: Umm, Lottie, you haven't taken your pills for six days?

BRUNO: Lottie, you're not allowed to have sex for a month!

FRANK: I thought it was two weeks?

LILLY: You misplaced your pills a week ago and started a new sheet. Did you actually check your make-up bag?

LOTTIE: Oh, here it is. Calm down, Papi, I have taken all of them. [Sending a photo of an up-to-date blister sheet.]

I shook my head and smiled. They were a mess, my family, all of them, and suddenly the silence didn't feel so bad. I picked up the rubbish off the floor, took it downstairs and made myself a cup of coffee. And then I went and made myself a little nest in bed next to Frank, who was snoring loudly, curled around a pillow like a very thin, overgrown child. I stroked his hair and smiled as he moved in his sleep, his breaths slow and steady, the drip machine pausing the silence every so often with a comforting bleep.

I suddenly thought how lucky I was because none of my worries mattered anymore. All those worries, all those plans, none of them made any sense when I was here, at home, and everything seemed so obvious. Right in front of me was a life that mattered. I needed to remember that.

Chapter Eighteen
Lilly

GOING BACK TO uni was never going to be fun, and my body had been screaming with exhaustion this morning when I'd rolled out of bed. I hadn't been to the gym in weeks, and my head was hurting with dehydration and, well. School. Ugh.

I missed everyone, but it was, in a way, nice to be back to normal. I loved when we went away with the Norwegians, and I loved when they came here. It just made things fun and different, and the whole family took on a different dynamic. It worked. We all worked in some messed-up way.

I was still exhausted, though—not surprisingly since I'd truly burnt the candle at both ends by the time Christmas was over. I'd needed the time with Maria. She always seemed to get my head screwed back on right. Thomas and I seemed to have found a new level of pseudo-friendship too. We'd run errands and pick up orders and bought wrapping paper, and then I'd spotted this adult toyshop and made Thomas squirm with embarrassment calling him Daddy all over the shop and begging for him to buy me kinky sex toys. Apparently, he and Frank used to shop there, and he refused to tell me what for, but then he'd still showed me and it was so inappropriate that we were both screaming with laughter. I have no idea what the shop assistant made of it, but it had been fun. Then Thomas had cried in the car on the way home, and I'd held his hand and cried too because sometimes those were just the things we needed, to let our emotions show on the outside so we could hold it together on the inside.

I'd seen a different side of Thomas, and despite the sadness, we'd had a good talk. He'd told me that life wasn't always easy, but that I should go and live it, not let things hold me back. Live in the now because once the now became the past, there was no changing it.

I knew what he meant, and I doubted he knew all my deep, dark secrets, but for a moment there, perhaps he did. Secrets were no good to anyone. I knew that.

I'd been in love with someone I could never have since I was a little girl. Yeah. Clever. I know. I'd fantasised and dreamed and wanted and needed and made up every fairy-tale ending in the world in my head. I knew I didn't stand a chance with Fredrik. He was just... Well. He'd always been the man of my dreams, my ideal boyfriend, the golden Prince Charming with the big smile. I fell in love with him, and he fell in love with my big brother. That was the story. End of.

It didn't help me as a hapless teenager, though. I'd sit on his lap and I'd hug him and he'd cry into my hair. It was never for me. It was all over Andreas, and I'd hold him and shush him and then we'd talk. A lot. He texted me and I texted him.

I'd always been in love with him, and I'd never told anyone because Andreas? Yeah? Talk about messed up. Well, I'd told Fredrik that I loved him when I was eighteen, just to get it off my chest. I wrote him this long, rambling message, spilling my guts out all over the floor. He rang me straight back and told me he loved me too and then talked about the weather.

I think I cried for a week. Bloody boys, fucking hell.

Which, of course, made my mind play back the awkward conversation we'd had on New Year's Eve, when Fredrik had grabbed me and then shoved my coat in my face and pushed me out the front door saying we were going for a walk.

"Where's Andreas?" I'd snapped, pulling my hat over my head.

"Asleep," he'd muttered and tied the laces on his boots, stomped his feet in the snow. Nodded his head at me like I was supposed to understand.

"Fucked him into oblivion again, I assume," I'd snarled. It was hard to be friendly when your heart was broken. That was me being over-dramatic, by the way. Like always.

We'd walked in silence for a while, dodging the big chunks of heavy snow that fell from the trees along the path down towards the forest.

"I love you, Lils, and I want you to be happy," he'd said.

"I will be. One day," I'd replied in not much more than a whisper.

"You're my baby sister, but you're also one of my best friends in the world. I've told you things I haven't told anyone else, ever. I've cried with you, and we've laughed and we've lived through all kinds of fucked-up drama. I know you and me are kind of messy at times, but I've tried to keep you sane, you have to understand that. I push you away sometimes so you will go and find someone to love. Someone who will love you back and treat you like a princess, because I want you to have that. I want someone to love you like I love Andreas. It's the best thing in the world to have someone hold your heart like that.

"I know." For once, I hadn't known what else to say to him.

"Lils, you need to open your eyes to the world. Love is not found on flipping Tinder."

"My friend Sabina just got married to a bloke she met on Tinder."

"Shut up for a second and let me speak. I need to say things."

Fredrik in a nutshell. Pedantic. Perfectionist. A life all planned out.

"You've been thinking about this all week, haven't you." I'd laughed because I knew what he was like. He'd probably made a PowerPoint presentation for me too, with a matching spreadsheet.

"Yup. I have notes on my phone, in case I miss any of the important points that I'm about to make." He'd laughed too and thrown his arm around my shoulders, and I'd let myself be hugged because...hugging. Okay?

"Talk, Fredrik." I'd sounded sterner than I'd intended, but I'd known it would be one of the most cringeworthy conversations of my life, so whatever.

"I want you to do something for me, Lils."

"Okay?"

"Next time you go to class, just sit in the auditorium and look around. Really look. Observe the people around you, one by one. Some people will stare back at you. A few will look bored. Some will be doing other things, texting and stuff, but then there will be someone, someone who will get caught in the act of looking at you. Following your gaze around the room, and when you look straight at them, they will look away. Blush. Pretend to be looking for a pen in their bag or something."

I sighed. "Nobody uses pens anymore, Fredrik." I had no idea where he was going with this conversation.

"Look. Just look, Lils. Because there will be someone, let's call him *Tom*. Tom will be sitting there with his heart in a knot, hoping that today will be the day you notice him. He'll be sitting there hurting on the inside because the love of his life doesn't even know he exists. He'll be blushing because he doesn't dare to speak to you, and he thinks even if he did, you would blank him."

"I'm not an arsehole," I'd muttered.

"No, you're not. But you're missing out on that wonderful thing called love. You need to fall in love, for real. Not walk around crushing on me for the rest of your life."

"I am not crushing on you!" I'd lied, a little too loudly to be convincing.

"You need to fall in love, Lils." He'd stopped and grabbed my face, pressing a small kiss to my forehead. "I love you, and I will love you forever, but we both know that Andreas is the love of my life, and I have never ever felt anything like what I feel for him for anyone else. I want that for you. I want you to fall in love to the point where you think you're going insane when that other person is not there in your arms."

"You can use pronouns, you know. I'm into dudes. Nothing wrong with girls, but you don't have to be all sensitive around me."

"Whatever." He'd smiled. "There's probably a Tom in that classroom, and you need to give him a chance."

"What if this Tom is butt ugly and I don't fancy him?"

"It doesn't always matter. Worst case? He's an idiot and you block him on Instagram. Or you might gain this quirky friend who will love you forever. You might break his heart and he will move on, and so will you. But he might also turn out to be the best thing that ever happened to you."

"So I need to go to class, and figure out who Tom is." I'd sighed and treated him to an eyeroll.

"Yes, you do." He'd grinned. "And you need to be my little sister, and you need to promise that I will get to hold an epic speech at your wedding telling the story of how I made you talk to Tom."

"Tom is a figment of your fucked-up imagination." I'd elbowed him in his ribs. Hard.

He'd elbowed me back.

I still had the bruise, and I rubbed it gently with my hand as I turned around in my seat.

We were only a half-full class, as always. European Tax Law wasn't the most popular course on campus. It wasn't my favourite either, but I'd always liked Maths, and numbers were my thing, so I was going for a degree in International Economics, like all the other losers in this room waiting for class to start.

LILLY: I'm looking. In class. Can't see this Tom dude anywhere.

FREDRIK: He's there. Keep looking.

LILLY: Stop it. You made this whole story up and now my head is fucked. I'm looking for people who don't exist anywhere but in your imagination.

FREDRIK: Perhaps. But wasn't it worth a shot?

LILLY: I'm scrolling through Tinder instead. At least the people on there are real.

He sent me a load of emojis that made me laugh. Poor Fredrik. He'd left a two-bedroom flat in California for a dump of a childhood room in Berlin that came equipped with my slob of a brother, and the poor dude still hadn't found a job. Not even an interview on the horizon, but then it had been the holidays, so his timing had truly sucked. Andreas was obsessed with finding a flat all of a sudden and had bought pots and pans for them. And they had matching mugs. Sickening. Truly. Now the two of them were going back to Oslo for a week in February, and there was talk of skiing, while I would be stuck here with my lectures and pathetic life.

This Fredrik thing had consumed me over the last couple of days, and to say I'd been devastated was an understatement. I had crushed on him. It had hurt like hell seeing him and Andreas. And the sex thing had stung. Yes, I had sex too, thank you very much. I wasn't dead. Sex was fun, and I liked guys. I had a few friends who would put out when I needed it, and a hook-up was always a good way to let off steam. They didn't mean anything. Nothing more than fun times and a bit of embarrassing regret the next morning. I was always careful, and sensible, but those guys had never been enough though. Fredrik had been right, I was a spoilt princess. That bit was totally true, and I wanted my fucking fairy tale.

So I did as he said and sat there like a fool, gazing around the room again, staring at people like I'd lost the plot. Some of them were familiar faces:

he guy from calculus class waved at me, and I stuck my tongue out at him. He had a girlfriend. I'd met her once too.

There were a few older students, a gaggle of girls at the back laughing, some preppy dude talking on the phone and those hot blokes who always wore ties. Stupid kids pretending to be all grown up. *Nobody wears a tie at uni, arseholes.*

Then all of a sudden I spotted him, and my heart jolted, which was like super stupid. I laughed out loud at myself, because for a second he was looking at me, I was quite sure. Staring. Then, as soon as I looked back up at him, he looked away and acted as if he was reading his laptop screen. Then he looked again and went bright red.

Oops.

God, this was stupid. I was behaving like a creep here. I pretended to text on my phone, and then I looked up again. Right at him.

He dropped his phone on the floor with an embarrassing clunk. *Caught in the act, dude.* He was definitely looking at me, and now he was dying on the inside, stuffing his laptop into his backpack ready to leave.

I couldn't let him. I had a point to prove, and nothing would make me happier than to send Fredrik a selfie of me and this Tom dude, and then I could kick him in the nuts next time I saw him. I was about to embarrass the fuck out of myself as I scrambled my things together and climbed over the next row of seats.

"Don't leave!" I almost shouted at the poor guy, throwing my bag down on the seat next to his.

"I...err. Sorry," he stuttered out.

He was kind of...normal. Blond hair falling heavy over his eyes, totally nerdy glasses, a nervous smile and long arms. He was wearing some kind of gamer T-shirt under his checked flannel shirt. I recognised the logo because; hello. *Brothers.* I had them.

"Your name isn't Tom, by any chance?" I asked and plonked myself down, staring at him like the stalker I was.

"No?" he said weakly. "Perhaps you're mistaking me for my brother, but he's called Robin." The guy looked a little terrified.

"Okay?" I rolled my eyes. Fucking Fredrik.

"I'm Lilly." I politely reached out to shake his hand.

"Carl," the Tom dude said. Oh, so, now I would have to stop calling him that in my head. Carl. Dude was Carl. Cool.

"Lilly," I said again to try to catch my breath. *Good conversation, Lilly.*

"Lilly Moretti-Fischer," he replied. "I know, I follow you on Insta."

Now he was blushing again, which got me all hot and bothered. WTF?

"I mean, not like in a stalking way, but your account is kind of fun. I loved all the pictures from Norway. Is that your boyfriend, the tall guy with the man bun?"

This Carl guy was way worse than me, talking at three hundred miles an hour with his face all red like he was seriously about to combust.

"Noooo," I replied casually. I hoped I sounded casual anyway. On the inside, I was a bit of a mess. "He's my brother's boyfriend. They are like seriously *in lurve.* Can't stop shagging. But that's a whole other story."

"You have an identical twin sister," he continued, sounding a little calmer now.

"Yes. Lottie. Much prettier than me. Studying IT." Deep sigh. I got this *all* the time.

"I have a twin brother, Robin. He used to be at uni here with me, but now he's dropped out and gone to France to do this big acting job. He's an actor. I tried it once too, got this part in a TV series, and only had six minutes of screentime. Then I got written out and dumped. That was it. End of story. So, now I'm going to be a piss-boring accountant instead. I might get to manage Robin's millions if I'm lucky. He's good. Sorry. I talk too much, can never control my mouth. I'm sorry."

"Don't apologise." I laughed. "You're just like me, always getting told that I talk too much. I can't shut up. It's a genetic defect, I think."

"It's cute," he said and then seemed to want to unalive himself from the inside again.

"You have a twin brother," I repeated, like this was brand-new information. It kind of was. I hadn't really taken it in when he'd said it.

"Yeah. We're identical too, which is why I thought you were mistaking me for him. I get that all the time. My brother is really cool and knows everyone."

"Never met your brother," I admitted, taking another deep breath. "Fredrik, that's my brother's boyfriend, he told me I had to do a challenge for him, to look around the room in my first class and find the guy called Tom who had a crush on me."

"My name is not Tom." He grinned again. Like I was funny. I wasn't. I was a fucking embarrassment.

"I know, but he said I had to look for the guy who was watching me, the one with the secret crush, who would be the man of my dreams. He said there was a guy somewhere who would be the love of my life and would make me fall in love. In class. Ridiculous, right?"

I stared at him, smiling back at me.

"I can tick the box for the crush," he admitted quietly. "You light up the room, and yeah. Sorry. I've been crushing on you for a while, but I know you're totally out of my league, and sorry about the staring. I like watching you. You're beautiful, I can't help it." He looked down, fiddling with the cover of his laptop.

"I..." What was I supposed to say to that?

"Class is about to start," he said, opening up his laptop. "You can leave me to die of embarrassment now."

"I have to stay," I lied. "Fredrik told me I had to sit next to you. I mean, I *have* to sit here because how else am I supposed to fall in love with you?"

"You could start by letting me buy you a coffee after this lecture, and then perhaps you could email me your notes because I won't be able to concentrate on anything Professor Helmut says with you sitting next to me. I mean. You're Lilly Moretti-Fischer."

"I'm good at notes. I like coffee," I mumbled weakly. Who was this dude? This total gamer nerd was flooring me with his totally nerdy perfection. Fuck you, Fredrik. FUCK YOU.

I got my phone out and texted Fredrik a load of angry emojis. He texted me love hearts back.

"I'm nobody. I can't even get a boyfriend," I whispered as this Carl guy tapped furiously at his laptop and stared intently at the lecturer, who had fired up his first slide on the large screen at the front of the auditorium.

"Class is starting. Take notes. I'm having a quiet freak-out here."

The dude's shoulders hitched up and down with his laughter.

"I have stupid friends with benefits. I'm tired of hook-ups. I have a crush on my brother's boyfriend. I'm a fucking mess, Carl. I need to grow up and fall in love. I need to be treated like a princess apparently. Well, that's what Fredrik said. I need someone to sweep me off my feet and kiss me in the morning, morning breath and all. My family is your worst fucking nightmare, and my twin sister will kill you if you hurt me. Any questions?"

I was smiling at his obvious struggle to stop himself laughing out loud.

"I'm the black sheep of my family, and my twin brother is a star," he whispered, still pretending he was listening to Professor Helmut yap on about Brexit. "I got six minutes of screentime. That was it. My acting career down the drain. I have a crush on the most beautiful girl in the world and she insists on sitting next to me in class. Bloody nightmare, this. Have you got anything to eat? Because I feel like I'm going to faint. Next thing, you'll be following me on Instagram and my life will be over."

"What's your handle?" I giggled and opened up the Instagram app on my phone. "Lilly's dreamboat?"

"Piss off." He giggled, gesturing at Professor Helmut droning on in front of us. "Lecture? Take notes."

I reached into my bag and fished out the small bag of Uncle Frank's biscuits that I had stashed there earlier this morning, picked one out with my fingertips and reached across so it was right in front of his mouth.

"Open wide," I whispered. "Don't faint. We need to listen to this. It's 'The impact of Brexit on European trade law'. It changed the laws of tax allowances in international trade quite dramatically. Very interesting. We can learn a lot from it."

He tried to say something back, but he was spitting biscuit crumbs and closing his eyes and doing all kinds of dreamy looks. Yeah, Uncle Frank's biscuits were kind of orgasmic, I could give him that.

"I'll take notes," I continued. "Just don't pass out. Then we're going for coffee later and I need to follow you on Insta. I want to see pictures of your brother. We need to talk. I mean, you're going to sweep me off my feet and make me fall in love, so we have to make some plans? Okay?"

I winked at him and fired up my laptop, pretending to be super interested in the lecture in front of us.

I could see him shaking his head and laughing next to me.

Whatever.

Fredrik 0 – Lilly 1.

Four Years Later

Chapter Nineteen
Lottie

To: <u>p.ansbacher@gmail.com</u>
From: <u>bookings@bellasfarm.se</u>
Re: Your booking at Bella's Farm

Dear Mr Ansbacher,

Thank you for your booking and the full payment for your four-week stay at The Barn apartment at Bella's Farm. We will be delighted to welcome you to our small piece of heaven here in the Swedish countryside.

Included in your stay is unlimited Wi-Fi on our lightning-fast fibre network, full access to our cable network of TV and streaming options, weekly cleaning and all bedding and towels for one person, as per your booking. You will find a welcome pack of basic groceries in your lodgings on arrival (please advise of any dietary restrictions), but we highly recommend you bring supplies or book a grocery delivery from <u>www.icahenriksvik.se</u> to be delivered at your convenience. There is no shop or catering facility on site.

The sauna and hot tub on the beach can be booked in advance on our website, and the gym facilities are in the same building as your accommodation. The gym is open 24/7. We are happy to provide running maps and details of local attractions on request. Laundry facilities available.

I PRESSED SEND, drained the last of my champagne and looked out at the garden in front of me—a garden that was filled with all the people I loved. It made me think back to that dreadful Christmas four years ago, the one where we had all tiptoed around on tenterhooks thinking Uncle Frank was about to pop his clogs and die with every raspy breath he'd taken.

I'd had a quiet word with him that Christmas Eve and told him if he died, I would kill him. Truly. Have him buried in some very unflattering clothing and ensure his coffin was painted in some ghastly green colour.

That had made him laugh. I'd made some more threats, and he'd just hugged me and whispered that he loved me.

He'd taken a turn for the worse that spring, which made Fredrik move back home for a month. My Vati had travelled to Oslo a few days later. Then come home again.

Frank was still here. He still wasn't in the clear, but the man running around on the lawn was in much better shape than he'd been back then. He was still thin and his once thick mop of hair had never recovered to its former glory, but he was still my uncle Frank, and he was still Uncle Thomas's husband and my Vati's best friend, and we were still this incredible family. Just thinking that made the hairs stand up at the back of my neck. I couldn't imagine losing anyone. Not now. Not here. And now Uncle Frank was picking up my daughter and throwing her up in the air.

Yeah. Hello. I'm Lottie Moretti-Fischer, and I was a fuck-up of epic proportions. The one who hadn't learned a thing from my parents' past mistakes. Instead, I was the one who'd made All-the-Mistakes™. Because that Christmas, when my family thought life was about to implode on them, was the Christmas when I'd shagged someone in the back of a club in Oslo and taken home more of a souvenir than I'd bargained for. I'd never even asked his name.

I'd pretended it wasn't happening for months, suffering with that kind of panic in your chest that made every day a struggle, where the lies built up and my health took a swing for me, and then my Papi had finally sat me down at the kitchen table and put his hand on my stomach and said, "Enough, Lottie. Enough."

I'd cried for an hour, and then we'd booked an appointment with the local antenatal clinic. Three months later, I'd given birth to Bella Moretti-Fischer.

I wish, dear reader, that that would have been the end of my troubles. But I was who I was, and I hadn't taken well to the role of motherhood. I'd lived in my childhood room and tried to grow up with this tiny alien being that constantly screamed in a basket next to my bed, where I'd spent most of my time crying. That I'd felt overwhelmed and judged and ill-equipped was a massive understatement. But like with everything, life had thrown me an odd turn and things had worked out. Well, Uncle Thomas and Uncle Frank had thrown me a lifeline, with a little help from Papi and Vati and some big streaming service that had decided that Bella's Farm was the perfect set-up for their big new production of *Celebrity Snowflake*. Yeah. I'd laughed too. They were going to send a bunch of Z-list celebrities with issues out to camp in the forest with no access to any mod cons, filming them twenty-four seven, and they were going to set up a full production facility on site, alongside planning permission to turn the barn and cabin into luxury accommodation and recreation facilities for the two B-list celebrities who would host the show.

Uncle Thomas had insisted on having someone live on site to keep an eye on things, and apparently, I was the woman for the job. With a baby in tow and my impeccable IT skills from my failed degree, this would give me an opportunity to go back to uni and study online, and on top of that I would get free accommodation and get paid. They'd dangled that like a carrot in front of me, when I'd already mentally packed my bags and was ready to leave. Anything to get away from the hell I'd landed myself in.

I'd laughed in their faces. Then cried. Then bought myself a little car with a loan from Fredrik and packed up my life and my screaming infant and driven to Sweden in some sleep-deprived zombie state.

As expected, my Vati cried himself into a stupor. Papi had popped some of his emergency pills and slept until I'd called to say I'd arrived. Well, I'd got lost a few times, but I'd made it in one piece, even staying in a swanky budget hotel halfway. Baby Bella had been surprisingly fabulous to handle and I'd somehow felt free, relieved, capable even, parking my car on the lawn in front of the house, narrowly swerving a fallen apple tree and finding that the roof was once again leaking and the electricity had tripped.

Capable, I had repeated to myself. *I am a grown-up, a parent. I am responsible and capable.*

I hadn't believed it then, and I still had moments where my confidence faltered. But in other moments, I looked at this farm, this place, and smiled at what I'd achieved.

I'd single-handedly pulled this place, kicking and screaming, into the current century, with a snazzy row of glamping tents and two new semi-permanent lodges on site plus the barn conversion with its pretty awesome raised veranda, and the renovated cabin now housed a private hot tub at the back. And the gym. And the updated sauna and hot tub on the beach. And the Wi-Fi, which these days kicked ass. All paid neatly for by the production team of *Celebrity Snowflake*, Season 3, and I'd just signed the contracts for Season 4 to roll in at the beginning of autumn.

Humans were crazy and had somehow taken to that show and then decided to come and find themselves in these mosquito-infested swamps, so I'd just jumped on the bandwagon, and now Bella and I ran quite the swanky operation here, happily buying into the show's tagline of there being *a little magic in between these trees.*

I'd already known there was, after the first year when I'd truly grown up. I'd worked harder than I ever had, my body aching at the end of every day. I'd never finished uni, but I'd well and truly enrolled in the school of life, dealing with everything from high-tech wiring for camera equipment and catering truck hygiene regulations to stuck-up production assistants who needed a reality check. And forestry. Because fuck, we had a lot of trees here, and apparently, they needed care and attention and cutting down, which both cost money and made money. Told you. I'd learned a lot.

The other thing I'd learned was that everything on TV was a total lie, I'd quickly figured that one out, hosting the poor celebrities and their phones and laptops in my kitchen at night while they cried on my shoulder and charged their tech from my burnt-out plugs, all with a baby hanging off my boob.

I'd made mistakes, of course, but I'd finally got my head together, enrolled Bella in day-care in Henriksvik three days a week and started working from the small community centre in the village, befriending the barista in the café and worming my way into the surprisingly vibrant bartering community that I'd never been aware of. Turns out I was quite the whizz with computers, could host both human guests and sheep on my land, and the farm had hunting rights to trade for fresh meat. Yes, Maria, my vegetarian ways went out the window because I was trying to live and provide and build a life, and the local hunters were more than happy to teach me what I needed to know, even though my Swedish language skills still sucked since everyone spoke English. I also had a multitude of autumn fruits that I picked, packed and bartered to ensure I had an endless free supply of coffee and café lunches. See? I was good at this shit. Really good.

I had builders and plumbers on call and an electrician who would check over my wiring every year and had hardwired my smoke alarms in return for my apparently excellent marketing skills and maintaining his website. I also had weekly grocery deliveries, a new accountant and humans who had become truly good friends.

I'd found myself being a mother. Fuck the world and all that. But I was starting to think that maybe one day I would kick ass at motherhood too. Bella was the light of my life, my little buddy, the one who hugged me and kissed me and made everything better when things seemed a little bleak.

I had a three-year-old daughter, and I was never having sex again. Ever. I wished someone had told me how hard it was to parent and be adult and how to financially thrive when every breath was draining your bank account, but I wouldn't change things for anything. Also, my parents *had* told me all of that; I just hadn't listened or understood. Now I did because Bella was a force and I was her mum, and I could honestly not ask for anything more in life than I already had here on this farm.

Especially now, this bright summer's day when we were all together again. My family. My Vati and Papi dressed up, Uncle Thomas with a phone pressed to his ear, no doubt trying to get directions through to the Humanist wedding officiant who was hopelessly lost somewhere north of Henriksvik. Maria was absolutely beautiful, standing next to Fredrik, who actually looked pretty good in a tux—even better than Carl, who had scrubbed up surprisingly well as best man. And Lilly, of course, my blooming, beautiful sister wobbling around on the uneven lawn in high heels trying to catch Bella. She made me laugh, and I wriggled my toes in my trainers, which I'd refused to change out of, even though I was reluctantly wearing a dress.

I loved the solitude here, having grown up with people constantly in my space. Loneliness was my new best friend, and I treasured her like a goddess. I loved this place. I loved my home, where I slept in what had once been Fredrik's room, while Bella had taken over Maria's. I'd left Thomas and Frank's bedroom well alone. Because. Yeah. They still owned the place and I had some respect, which they showered me with in return when they came to stay, and they often did. I loved that. My parents came twice a year, and my siblings seemed to randomly appear, squeezing themselves in between bookings and putting their noses in my business like only siblings could. I was never lonely. Ever.

"Remember the first summer here?" my brother asked like he was talking to nobody in particular. I'd not even realised he'd come into the kitchen, grabbed a glass of water and sat at the table. Pushing my laptop away, he gave me a stern look. "No working!" He wagged his finger at me. "It's my wedding day, and we're supposed to party."

"Can't believe you're getting married. And that Lils beat you to it."

"I was so pissed off at that. I had to propose, just out of spite," he lied, laughing. "But seriously. Remember that first summer here?"

"Yes." I had memories. I'd just been a small child, but I'd heard enough stories to make that summer stand out. "I almost drowned somewhere and tried to set something on fire and got chicken pox on the ferry home."

"Yes. All of that is probably true. But a lot of things changed that summer. Vati and Papi changed. Things were different when we got home, and I always thought it was them who had changed. Now I think I changed too. Maybe I remember things differently, but I truly think fate was at play. I mean, look at us. If it hadn't been for that holiday, none of us would have ended up where we are today." He drew with his fingers on the tabletop.

I drew too—a breath—and let it go with a giggle. "You're such a dork."

"I know." He smiled. "Spent years trying to be someone I never was. And now...this is me. Bad haircut. Bad skin. Stupid ideas. Good tux, though."

"Very good tux." I reached out and traced his sleeve. He looked good. Smart. Happy. "Freddie looks good too. You've got one hell of a handsome dude on your hands."

"I know." He grinned smugly. "Isn't he just...brilliant?"

I sighed.

"We need to find Maria a partner," Andreas said. "I hate that she's still single."

"Maybe we need not find Maria a partner?" I suggested. "Maria is fine. She's a headteacher. She doesn't want kids. She's happy and bloody brilliant. Not everyone has to be like you. Married. Volvo. Dog. House. Two point four kids."

"Are you calling me a statistic?"

"Yeah. And get off Maria's back. Some of us are just content and happy as we are. Sometimes not following those generic formulas is the right path to take, and Maria is making a difference to the world in her own way. I love that she's happy."

"I suppose you're right."

"I am. You nervous?" His smile told me the answer.

"No. Not a bit. I mean, Freddie and I...we're good. This marriage thing and the paperwork and stuff is just something that will make things simpler. We want to have kids. Build a house. Make sure we're looked after in our old age and all that crap."

"None of that is important. Look at me. No property, a kid and not a marriage certificate in sight."

"Yeah, you're a total loser, sis." He snorted. He didn't mean it. Or maybe he did.

"It's nice that it's just us. I don't think I could have coped with hosting a load of your mates too."

"Says the woman who runs a fully booked holiday site."

We both chuckled, a comfortable silence once again filled the room.

"I'm not worried about you," he said, "despite Vati and Papi always telling me that I should be. You're the lucky one. All this freedom and no pressure to be anything else than what you are. A good businesswoman. A mother. A thinker. And you rule this little kingdom full of magic like you're some kind of fairy queen. Even the mosquitoes have stayed away today."

"Put a few spells out, me." I winked. "This place is full of magic. You know it."

"Now you've started to believe in your own hype."

"I do believe in my own hype. This place got featured in *Amelia* magazine last week, 'Top Ten Most Magical Staycations'. We're fully booked until next year now."

"Oh, look at you!" he teased.

"I still let you have your honeymoon here. For free. I might charge you next year."

"You wouldn't dare."

I would. I wasn't having any of his freeloading. "What were you saying about that first summer here again?"

"That I hated being cut off. The silence. The bloody nature thing. I really hated it here, almost the whole first week. Now? I can't think of a place I love more. I come here and life slows down. My thoughts seem to work better and all that stress just disappears. Then—"

"Bullshit." I cut him off. "You want to take a look at my accounts and your blood pressure will go straight through this roof. At least it doesn't leak anymore."

"Says the woman who made a massive profit last year."

"All of which got reinvested in the business. Apart from that, I bought a better backup generator and changed Bella's car seat."

"I know," he said, then mumbled something I couldn't understand.

"Speak up, dork," I scolded and stared at him.

"Freddie and I were thinking."

"Thinking is dangerous, especially for you two."

"We were thinking. Perhaps building our own home from scratch in Berlin is wrong. Freddie works from home anyway, and I want to have kids. I've already thought about consultancy work, and I could do that from anywhere."

"Oh fuck," I blurted out, but I was smiling.

"Freddie didn't dare ask, so here I am doing his dirty work."

"Coward." I giggled. "I knew I shouldn't have mentioned it to you, but now you want to buy the land up for sale, don't you? The bit along the water further up. The land I was going to bid on. And you're going to totally gazump me and ruin my brilliant plans for a proper campsite."

"The land you've been talking about for the last six months?" He grinned. "Lotts, you are brilliant, which is why we thought that perhaps that is where we should build this house of ours. Fuck the campsite. Who wants a load of holidaymakers up there anyway? No, we thought we'd move up here, have a bunch of kids, live the good life and...and also? You could have a break. Go on holiday. Have some cocktails on a beach somewhere for a change."

"My very worst nightmare would be going on some godforsaken holiday filled with humans and alcohol and...fuck. I think you just trumped that one. My worst nightmare would be having the two of you as neighbours. Fuck, Andreas. Nope. Never."

I was lying through my teeth. Of course I was. But Freddie was not genetically coded for country life, and Andreas would lose his shit within weeks, and me? I would no doubt kill them both.

"You're not serious," I almost growled out.

"You are superwoman. You can do this by yourself, we all know that, but I won't let you. This is our family, and we've never been able to do things on our own. If Freddie and I don't get ourselves building a house now, we'll never leave Berlin. Freddie will start wearing lederhosen and take up smoking a pipe, and I will lose my shit at him. We need to start living, properly. I want to come here, and...I mean. You're the boss. This is your gig, and I would never interfere."

"Says the guy who threw me and my baby out of the house."

He laughed. "I simply carried you out because our parents wouldn't let go of you, both of them convinced you would drive yourself to a certain death before even hitting the autobahn."

Another truth.

"So, you're getting married, then moving here and taking over my house while you build some modern monstrosity that you will never get planning permission for and I'll have to live with you for the rest of my life?"

"You will have to live with me and my enormously gorgeous husband for the rest of your life. And Bella will have some super cool uncles to hang out with. And cousins."

"Lils is four months pregnant. Bella will have a cousin already."

"Our kids will be cooler cousins. And we'll have a dog."

"Carl is allergic."

"Carl can go fuck himself. I want a dog."

"Carl already fucked Lils and got her up the duff."

He smiled and took my hand. "Stop it," he said softly. "I'm serious. I want this, but I don't want to step on your toes. If you tell us no, we won't push it. But Freddie and I are absolutely serious. We think it would be good, you know? And then we would be closer to Frank and Thomas, and Vati and Papi would come up all the time. I mean, the airport is just two hours away. It's not like they have to drive these days."

"I know," I said, and I meant it as I leant over and gave my handsome brother a hug. "So, you're getting married today. In the garden."

"I am indeed. To the love of my life."

"And then you and Freddie are going to build yourself a house."

"Yup."

"And you need me to project-manage the whole thing while you two figure out how to live in the sticks without poking your eyes out with fencing poles."

"Something like that."

"Good."

"Good?"

"I can deal. Just don't piss me off because I don't take well to people having their nose in my business. I'll talk to the landowner and get you a fair deal on that land, and you will sit on your hands and let me get the paperwork in place before you do anything else. Clear?"

"Clear," he said, and I leant forward again.

"And you will be happy," I whispered. "Because you deserve it."

"I know," he whispered back.

I winked.

"And there *is* a little bit of magic in these woods. It's all true. You'll see. I'll make sure of it."

To: bookings@bellasfarm.se
From: p.ansbacher@gmail.com
Re: Your booking at Bella's Farm

Dear L Moretti-Fischer,

Thank you for the confirmation of my booking. I look forward to my stay. As per your question of my intentions with this holiday, I don't know how to answer that myself without sounding like, pardon the pun, a snowflake.

My wife of five months walked out on me a year ago, and I've finally managed to sell our flat. For years I have been working in a profession I simply don't understand and will never excel at. What I am saying is that it's time for a change, to make or break. I have put all my belongings into storage and intend to spend the coming weeks figuring out what on earth I am supposed to do with my life.

I'm not going to lie and say I haven't seen that TV show, where people claim your establishment has changed their lives, because I have. But I'm a reasonable human being and I just want peace and quiet. I intend to run, make use of your gym equipment and try to learn to cook something that doesn't come straight from a packet.

But most of all I want to learn to live with myself. With my choices and mistakes. With my uncertain future and perhaps, in between those trees and the lake, I can figure out where to go from here. Because I think somewhere, there is a future for me too. I just need to find it.

Thank you for your kindness, and I will see you next week.

Pierre Ansbacher

Dedicated to everyone still fighting.
And in memory of those who bravely fought.

About the Authors

Magdalena Di Sotru is an information security and data protection enthusiast from Norway. She is a mother of two and wife of one as well as a long-established fanfic writer. Her favourite food is (actually) salads (without mayo), her favourite guilty pleasure is fresh bakery goods (and that explains why everyone would think the salad was a lie). She knows her way around knitting, lock picking and skydiving (all at about equal skill levels – go figure). Life is Good and Other lies was her first novel.

Sophia Soames should be old enough to know better but has barely grown up. She has been known to fangirl over TV shows, has fallen in and out of love with more popstars than she dares to remember, and has a ridiculously high-flying (un-)glamourous real-life job.

Her long-suffering husband just laughs at her antics. Their children are feral. The dogs are too.

She lives in a creaky old house in rural London, although her heart is still in her native Scandinavia.

Discovering that the stories in her head make sense when written down has been part of the most hilarious midlife crisis ever, and she hopes it may long continue.

Linktr.ee/sophiasoames

717 Miles
717 Miles Christmas

The Scandinavian Comfort Series
Little Harbour
Open Water
Baking Battles

In this Bed of Snowflakes We Lie
The Naked Cleaner

The Chistleworth series
Custard and Kisses
Ship of Fools
This Thing with Charlie

The London Love Series
BREATHE
EXHALE
TASTE
SLEEP (coming soon)
SKIN and BONES (coming soon)

Force Majeure
Life is Good and Other Lies
Life is Right Here

Short stories
What If It All Goes Right
Honest